## "But you did know she left her husband."

Nick's face was without expression. "I only heard a couple of days ago."

"Does she still attract you?" Lauren's question came without volition, drawing a faint satirical smile from Nick. She was silent for a moment before continuing, "I won't have you coming to me from another woman!"

His gray eyes glittered. "How would you know?"

"I'd know." She drew in a shaky breath. "Promise me you won't see her again, or we call off the wedding ceremony altogether!"

"Then you'd better get on with it." His gaze penetrated her soul. "I don't care for ultimatums. We've shared many fine moments. No doubt we could share many more, given the opportunity."

"But you won't give me your word?"

"No."

# Books by Kay Thorpe

## HARLEQUIN PRESENTS

## HARLEQUIN ROMANCE

These books may be available at your local bookseller.

Don't miss any of our special offers. Write to us at the following address for information on our newest releases.

Harlequin Reader Service
P.O. Box 52040, Phoenix, AZ 85072-2040
Canadian address: P.O. Box 2800, Postal Station A,
5170 Yonge St., Willowdale, Ont. M2N 6J3

# KAY THORPE

## no gentle persuasion

*Harlequin Books*

TORONTO • NEW YORK • LONDON
AMSTERDAM • PARIS • SYDNEY • HAMBURG
STOCKHOLM • ATHENS • TOKYO • MILAN

Harlequin Presents first edition May 1985
ISBN 0-373-10789-7

Original hardcover edition published in 1984
by Mills & Boon Limited

Printed in U.S.A.

# CHAPTER ONE

BRIGHT sunlight beckoned invitingly through the large office window. Lauren stirred restlessly, glancing at her watch for the fourth time in as many minutes. Catching the movement, her father's secretary summoned an oddly strained smile.

'I'm sure they won't be much longer,' she said. 'Mr Brent will be wanting his lunch too, I imagine.'

Not with any desperation, thought Lauren dryly, returning the smile. Their own table had been booked for one, and it was gone twelve-thirty already. Michael, the headwaiter, would save it, of course, but the relaxing pre-luncheon drink would be out. Darn the man turning up out of the blue like this!

Not just anybody though, she was bound to acknowledge. One of the Company directors no less. Carol professed not to know the reason he was here, yet the strained look around her eyes and mouth seemed to have increased over the past twenty minutes. It was time her father took the plunge and married the woman, Lauren reflected, mind temporarily diverted. Ten years was long enough for a man to be alone. At forty, Carol Gordon was just right for him, and she certainly made no secret of her regard. They had been lovers for at least twelve months; that much Lauren knew for a fact. Sometimes she wondered if perhaps she herself was the stumbling block, yet had so far found no opportunity to put the question. Not that it seemed likely when she and Carol got along so well, but who was to know how others thought about things?

Taking that job in Brussels for a couple of years might prove to be a good idea in more ways than one. She wasn't even sure why she had hesitated at all. Everything else aside, at twenty-three it was time she began to see a little more of the world. One more month and she would be away.

If she lasted that long, she thought, coming back to the present and the pangs of hunger making themselves felt with ever-increasing emphasis. She had skipped breakfast in order to take an earlier train to town. With a morning's shopping behind her, and no more than a cup of coffee inside her, the very thought of food was enough to start her saliva glands working.

'I'm starving!' she declared plaintively, getting to her feet and crossing to the desk. 'Can't you think up some excuse to get the time across to those two in there, Carol?'

'Mr Brent said they weren't to be disturbed for any reason,' replied the older woman tonelessly. 'They can't be much longer.'

'You said that five minutes ago,' Lauren reminded her. She studied the other face with suddenly narrowed green eyes. 'There's something wrong, isn't there? You're all on edge. What's going on?'

'I don't . . .' began the latter, then broke off in some obvious relief as the inner office door opened, coming to her own feet. 'You're leaving, Mr Brent?'

'Apparently.' The voice was deep timbred, the tone faintly ironic. 'I think Mr Devlin might like a cup of strong black coffee.'

Lauren had swung to face the newcomer, standing with the base of her spine pressed lightly against the desk edge as she met the steely grey regard. He was younger than she would have imagined—no more than the mid-thirties—and a good six feet in height, with a lean, muscular frame beneath the superbly cut grey suit. In that fleeting moment the chiselled features and smoothly styled black hair imprinted an indelible image on her brain.

'I'm Lauren Devlin,' she said. 'Is my father not well?'

His smile was thin, detracting from the hint of sensuality in his lower lip. 'I doubt if he's feeling a hundred per cent right this moment, but the cause isn't organic.'

'Why?' The word was a demand. 'What happened?'

'Get him to tell you about it,' came the equally short reply. 'I'm already late.'

She caught a subtle scent of aftershave as he passed her on his way to the outer door. It took all her willpower to resist the urge to grasp that tailored sleeve and demand a more detailed explanation of his meaning. Carol was the first to move, making for the office where the man they both loved still silently resided. Lauren followed her in haste.

Hugh Devlin sat with his chair turned outwards to the view over the city rooftops, the balding patch on the top of his greying head clearly visible. He made no effort to move his position on their entry, looking from one face to the other with pain-filled eyes as they stepped round into his line of vision.

'I've been a fool,' he said. 'I thought I could get away with it.'

'It's the Clayfield account, isn't it?' asked Carol gently. 'They ran a spot check.'

Hugh stared at her. 'You knew?'

'I suspected,' she acknowledged. 'I knew you'd bought into that stock after you'd admitted to not having enough backing, and you've been edgy every time the account's been mentioned this last few months.'

'Would one of you mind explaining what you're talking about?' asked Lauren worriedly.

Her father shifted his gaze, brown eyes meeting green with weary acceptance. 'There's no point in trying to keep it from you. I borrowed a large sum of money in order to make a killing on a certain deal believing I'd have ample time to straighten things out before any audit was due. I'm not excusing myself. It was wrong, and I knew it, only the opportunity was too good to miss.' He paused, spreading his hands. 'I got caught. It's as simple as that. I gambled and I lost.'

It was Carol who voiced the obvious question. 'What are they going to do?'

The shrug came heavy. 'The only thing they can do. I have the weekend to straighten out my personal affairs, then it's in the hands of the police.'

'No!' The word was jerked from Lauren's lips, the full redness of the latter emphasising her pallor. 'They can't do that!'

Her father smiled faintly and shook his head. 'They have just cause. I betrayed a trust.'

'For the first time in more than twenty years. Surely that means something?'

He said softly, 'Bless you for taking it for granted it is the first time. That means a lot to me.'

Lauren dropped to her knees at the side of his chair to put her lips to his cheek. 'Everyone is allowed one mistake surely!'

'Not this size,' he returned ruefully. 'The worst of it is I'd have been home and dry in another three weeks— although that wouldn't have made me any better than I am either.'

Lauren sat back on her heels to view him with slightly parted lips. 'You mean you'd be able to pay back the money as soon as that? All of it?'

He nodded. 'And more, if compensation would help.'

'But it's surely to everyone's benefit if you're allowed to do just that?'

'Not the way Nick Brent sees it.'

'Are you saying he's the only one who knows about it so far?' Carol broke in shrewdly.

'He's the one who did the spot check,' acknowledged the man in the chair. 'Seems he likes to spend his evenings running stuff through the computer just for the practice. It was sheer luck he chose the Clayfield account. I have to be grateful he didn't have me run in right away. He'll be breaking it to the Board Monday morning.'

'Before or after he makes it a police matter?'

'Does it matter? He has power enough. They'll accept whatever action he recommends.'

'But he's keeping it to himself over the weekend?' insisted Lauren, a hazy plan already forming in her mind.

'That's the impression he gave me.' Hugh swung his chair back to face his desk, dropping his head into his hands. 'Just give me a minute or two on my own,' he said on a muffled note.

Carol put her hand on Lauren's arm when the latter hesitated, jerking her head in the direction of the door. Lauren went with her because there was little she could do if she stayed, looking at the other woman with hardening intent as the door closed between them and the man left inside.

'Do you have his private address?'

Carol wasted no time in asking who she meant. 'It won't do you any good,' she said on a hollow note. 'He isn't the kind of man to listen to pleas for clemency when he's already made up his mind.'

'But you do know where he lives?'

'I know where he stays when he's in town. He does a lot of travelling.'

'A pity he couldn't have stayed away a few weeks longer then.' Lauren caught the glance Carol gave her and smiled wryly. 'Yes, I know Dad's in the wrong, but he isn't the first to give way to a momentary temptation, and sending him to prison isn't going to help anybody. It would kill him. You have to realise that. He couldn't bear to be shut away!'

'It may not come to that,' Carol protested halfheartedly. 'As a first time offender. . . .'

'He'll be made an example of,' Lauren stated. 'This Brent man will see to that!'

'In which case you'll be wasting your time pleading with him.'

'But I still have to try.' Lauren steeled herself. 'Give me the address, Carol.'

'He won't be there, will he? He just said he had another appointment.'

'So I'll simply wait till he does get back.'

'And tell your father what?'

'The truth. He won't like it, but if there's any chance at all he has to grasp it.' It took a real effort to keep her tone steady. 'Please, Carol.'

The other sighed and went over to a filing cabinet. 'Rather you than me. He's a hard nut to crack, by all accounts.'

Lauren took the card handed to her, scarcely glancing at the words printed on it. 'Thanks. Just look after him for me till I get back, will you?'

'I'll look after him for both of us,' came the soft reply.

The sunlight which had seemed so bright and beckoning not half an hour ago failed to lighten Lauren's heart. Sitting in the taxi taking her to the

Knightsbridge address, she tried to think out her approach, failing miserably because there was no set of rules governing a situation like this one. If he'd gone to lunch she was probably going to have a long wait anyway, yet to be right there on the spot was the only sure way of catching him at all. Perhaps a good meal might even mellow him a little. It was a forlorn hope, and she knew it. The man she had met back there in the office would not be so easily swayed.

Her destination proved to be one of the palatial modern apartment blocks springing up wherever there was building space within the city limits. Her taxi driver lingered long enough to watch her mount the broad stone steps to the front entrance before moving off. Accustomed to that kind of attention, Lauren paid no heed. She could see her own reflection in the darkened, one-way glass of the double doors, her body curves smoothly outlined by the slim sheath of her pale green dress, red-gold hair curving inwards to frame finely moulded features. Lauren had no false modesty regarding her looks; too many people had made her aware of them. What irked her so badly was the failure of most to bother plumbing beneath the outer casing to the person within. Show the average man a pair of shapely legs and well-rounded breasts, and he had but one thought in mind!

A uniformed commissionaire sat at a table in the spacious, marble-floored lobby. Mr Brent was out, he declared, without bothering to consult the list at his elbow. No, he had no idea when he might be back. He smiled and lifted his shoulders when Lauren said she would wait, a knowing look in his eyes. She had the feeling she wasn't the first female to come searching for Nicholas Brent in this manner, though the circumstances could hardly have been the same. With no way of making her own position clear she would just have to grin and bear the innuendo in that smile, she decided fatalistically, accepting the man's invitation of a seat within the lobby area and a magazine to while away the time. Nothing mattered so long as she got to her quarry before Monday morning. She would even camp right here in the lobby if necessary to achieve that end.

By four o'clock when he did finally put in an appearance she was beginning to wonder if she really might have to spend the night here. The sight of the tall, powerful figure coming in through the swing doors gave rise to a whole tumult of emotions, swiftly dampened down. From her seat by one of the wide pillars, she watched the commissionaire intercept him, saw the movement of the latter's lips and the brief nod of his head in her direction, then the newcomer was coming towards her and she was rising nervelessly to her feet.

The expression in the grey eyes was anything but reassuring. Lauren found her gaze drawn inexorably to his mouth, registering the hard, unyielding line. Yet she hadn't expected it to be easy, had she? Appealing to this man's mercy would be useless. What she had to do was persuade him to see a better way of dealing with the situation.

His first words were curt. 'Did your father send you?'

'No, he didn't!' she denied.

'But he knows you're here?'

That stopped her, but only for a moment. 'He may do by now,' she admitted. 'It depends what Carol told him. What difference does it make? It was all my own idea.'

'With the aim of getting me to change my mind?' He shook his head, lip curling faintly at the look in her eyes. 'No chance.'

'You haven't given *me* a chance yet,' she claimed

desperately. 'You could at least listen to what I have to say before you turn me out!'

He eyed her for a moment in silence, taking in the spots of colour burning high on her cheekbones. She knew his glance would drop next to her breasts, but in her present state of mind she could no more have stilled the agitated breathing that was making them rise and fall so noticeably than fly. Her colour had deepened by the time he looked up again, but she refused to flinch from the cynicism in his regard. He could think what he liked; she wasn't putting anything on. Right now she felt almost physically sick with the sheer effort of carrying this thing through.

'All right,' he said, 'so you'd better come on up and get it off your chest. Only don't count on anything. I'm not noted for going back on a decision.'

The fact that he was even bothering to warn her was a comfort of an odd kind. There had to be a first time for everything. Lauren accompanied him across to the lifts, aware of the frank interest of the man at the desk. His impressions were only too apparent, yet that scarcely mattered either. She had a foot in the door, so to speak. The rest was up to her.

The apartment was on the fifth and top floor, with a magnificent view over the park. A broad balcony ran the full width of the lounge, reached via sliding glass doors. Lauren had a vague impression of white upholstery and warmly gleaming woodwork, but her mind was on other matters.

'Sit down,' Nick Brent invited. 'I imagine you could do with a drink?'

Lauren had no particular liking for alcohol normally; today, however, was different. 'May I have a gin and tonic?' she asked, taking a seat in one of the huge deep chairs by the mock fireplace.

'Sure. I'll have one too.'

The bar was set into a corner of the big living room. Lauren kept her eyes averted while he mixed the drinks, listening to the clinking of glasses with a growing conflict inside her. A part of her wanted desperately to get up and leave this place now, while the going was good, yet the need to press her father's case was strong enough to make that course of action difficult. This man was going to need a lot of persuading to even consider a change of mind, and she had a very good idea of the form that persuasion might be expected to take. The look in his eyes downstairs just now hadn't been new to her; she had seen it before, too many times. The question was, if it came right down to it, would she be prepared to go through with it?

Remembering the agony in her father's eyes, she knew the answer had to be yes, providing the outcome was guaranteed first. Anything had to be better than a jail term for the man she loved.

The drink was stronger than she was accustomed to. Lip curling, she took a long swallow, controlling the urge to gag and choke by sheer effort of will. She didn't need to be drunk to do what she was planning to do, but a certain numbness wouldn't be unwelcome. He had perched himself on the arm of a sofa at right-angles to where she sat; she could feel his eyes on her. When she looked up at him it was with a forced directness.

'It will save a lot of time if I tell you I'm prepared to do anything you want to get my father off the hook. All *I* want is your promise that you'll give him the chance to put things right.'

There was a pause before he answered; the grey eyes were unreadable. 'Aren't you rather jumping the gun?' he asked at length without particular inflection. 'I'll grant you're a very desirable young woman, but. . . .'

'But you're not that kind of man, is that what you're going to tell me?'

His smile was slow. 'I'd not say that. How old are you, anyway?'

'Over the age of consent,' she responded smartly.

'And a damned little cynic to boot.' He looked at her for a moment with narrowed gaze, then shrugged and leaned forward to put down his glass on the table at her side. 'Okay, so let's get to it. I don't have too much time to spare.'

It was what she had expected—what she had asked for in effect—yet the actuality was still a shock. She stared at him without moving, fingers clasped so hard about the cold glass that the skin showed white at her knuckles. 'Just like that?' she got out.

He put out a hand and took the glass from her, depositing it on the same table before drawing her to her feet. This close he was whole inches above her, his mouth level with her eyes. There was ruthlessness in the set of his lips, making her shiver inwardly.

'How else would you expect me to handle it?' he asked brusquely. 'You made me an offer, I accept. Why waste any time?'

'You're forgetting one thing,' Lauren came back, trying not to flinch from the feel of those strong fingers on her skin. 'I want your assurance regarding my father first.'

His laugh jolted her. 'Cash on delivery, that's my idea of a deal—and only then if the goods are worth the price. Come and show me what you can do, then we'll talk about it.'

'No!' She hit out at him, only to find herself swung off balance as he turned her bodily across the room. Propelled ahead of him, it was all she could do to keep on her feet.

A door loomed ahead. Through it they were in a bedroom, the semi-circular bed set against the far wall on a raised dias. Still dragging her feet, Lauren felt herself lifted and carried the last couple of yards to be tossed face down on the navy spread. She rolled immediately, using an elbow as a prop as she stared up at the man standing over her.

'You're a cheat!' she got out. 'I shouldn't have expected any better!'

'True,' he agreed, totally unmoved. 'You came here expecting to get laid, and laid you're going to be!'

She was motionless as he shed his jacket and loosened his tie, mind gone totally numb. She could scream rape, of course, but who was going to believe her? The commissionaire downstairs could testify to her insistence on this meeting.

'You won't enjoy it,' she promised, tearing her eyes away from the bronzed and muscular torso to look directly into the hard eyes. 'I won't lift a finger to fight you, if that's what you're hoping for!'

'The proverbial ice-maiden?' His fingers were at his belt, easing the leather through the buckle. 'We'll see, shall we?'

It took the soft burr of the telephone beside the bed to still his movements. For a fleeting moment he remained standing there looking at her, as if weighing the possibility of simply ignoring the summons, then he shrugged and let the belt lie.

'Saved by the bell,' he said cynically. 'I wasn't expecting that call for another ten minutes. You'll excuse me if I take it in the other room.'

Lauren pushed herself slowly upright as he left the room, running a hand over her hair in an automatic effort to tidy her appearance. Her shoes had come off in that final struggle to escape his arms, lying where they had fallen. Putting them on again she felt safer, though no less sick. The whole scheme had been crazy from the start. This man wasn't going to let her father off the hook, no matter what incentive was offered to him. Had that call not come through at such an opportune moment he would have used her without compunction and probably thrown her out right afterwards. He still might if she didn't get herself together before his return.

He was still on the phone when she opened the door, standing with his back to her across the width of the room. Resisting the urge to run, Lauren walked over and picked up her handbag from the chair where she had left it, then made for the outer lobby. Nick was speaking rapidly, and not in English. He hadn't even turned his head in her direction. Finding the outer door locked and the key absent came as a shock she could not at first assimilate. She stood there with her hand on the knob simply staring at it.

Behind her the receiver was replaced. 'Not as easily as that,' he said softly. 'I have the key right here. If you want it, come and fetch it.'

Lauren turned on the spot, her back coming up against the smooth wood. His bare chest was covered in dark hair, his stomach ridged with muscle where the waistband of his trousers fitted. His belt buckle still hung open the way he had left it, the clip beneath needing but a flick of one finger to release it.

'I changed my mind,' she said with what pride she could muster, and saw one dark brow lift.

'Meaning your father isn't worth the sacrifice after all?'

'Meaning I wouldn't trust you to keep any promise you made even if you made it,' she responded bitterly. 'I was a fool to come here at all!'

'You were a fool to imagine a quick lay might be all

that was needed to get me to change my mind,' came the sardonic comment. 'Did you really think I was so short of a woman?'

Teeth gritted, she said, 'I don't imagine you go short of anything much. I didn't have any other incentive to offer, that's all.'

'You could have tried a simple request for starters.'

She looked at him, sensing the irony. 'Would it have done any good?'

'Maybe not, but you weren't to know that for sure.'

'I suspected it. Carol warned me you'd be a difficult man to convince.'

'Carol being?'

'My father's secretary.'

'Ah, yes, the devoted Miss Gordon. For all I know she's involved in this thing too.'

'She had nothing to do with it,' Lauren defended. 'My father will tell you the same.'

'The word of a criminal?'

'Don't call him that!' Her tone was sharp with anger and resentment. 'You've no right!'

'I've every right. He stole money.'

'He'll return every penny given half a chance—with interest too!'

His lips twisted. 'Ill-gotten gains? That's a rare offer!'

The tension in her drained suddenly, leaving her dully resigned. 'There's little point in continuing this conversation, is there? Just open the door and I'll stop wasting your valuable time.'

He studied her without moving, gaze travelling the length of her body with slow deliberation, lingering on the line of her thigh beneath the thin sheath, following the curve of her hip into slender waist and on up to the swell of her breasts. Something in his expression underwent an indefinable change. 'Time is what we're talking about. From what your father said earlier, he needs a few weeks.'

'Three, to be exact.' Lauren was cautious, scarcely believing what he appeared to be suggesting. 'I'd want it in writing first.'

Grey eyes hardened again. 'I'm afraid my word will have to be good enough.'

She had to trust him, Lauren thought desperately. She had no other choice. She took a deep breath, fighting for the nerve to see her through. 'All right, I'll take your word.' It was an effort to stand away from the door, to don the expressionless mask. 'To use your own words, let's get to it.'

'You don't listen very well, do you?' The tone was mocking. 'I already told you a quick lay wasn't going to be enough. I leave for Rome on Tuesday morning. That should give you ample time to pack.'

She said slowly, 'I don't understand. What. . . .'

'You're not dim-witted. Still, if you must have it spelled out for you. . . .' He paused, watching her face with that same mocking little smile on his lips. 'I do a lot of travelling, most of it alone. This trip I fancy a companion. All expenses paid, of course.'

She stared at him, mind searching frantically for a way out. He meant every word, that was obvious. 'You can't possibly expect me to go along with that kind of arrangement,' she got out at last. 'As you said, you're hardly likely to go short of a woman.'

'There's women and women. I like the idea of taking my own along.'

'Pre-programmed to serve your every whim, I suppose?' She fought down any tendency in her voice to tremor. 'Apart from anything else, I have a new job to go to at the beginning of next month.'

'It's only the second of this month,' he pointed out,

unmoved. 'You'll be back home by the twenty-eighth at the latest.'

'Always assuming I'm going to say yes in the first place.'

He looked at her for a calculated moment. 'You know the alternative.'

She bit her lip. 'That's blackmail!'

'Is there so much difference between that and bribery?' He shook his head as she opened her mouth to voice further protest. 'Take it or leave it—only make your mind up quickly before I go off the whole idea.'

'I'll take it.' There was little else she could say under the circumstances.

'Good.' He glanced at the thin gold watch circling one tanned wrist. 'I'm going to have to get moving. I'll phone down and ask George to get you a taxi.'

'I can get my own taxi.' Her mind felt numb. 'What do I tell my father?'

'That's up to you. The truth, if you think he can take it.'

'It's a test, isn't it?' Lauren said suddenly. 'You want to know if he's the kind of man who'd go along with anything to save his own skin. If I told him the truth there'd be no question!'

'So don't.' He was beginning to sound impatient. 'You made the choice, you're stuck with it. I want you round here with your bags packed ready to go by Monday evening, or we go right back to square one. Now, let's see about that taxi.'

Lauren waited until he had completed the call downstairs before giving voice to her thoughts. 'Did anyone ever tell you,' she said bitterly, 'that you're a complete bastard?'

'It's been known.' There was a certain irony about his mouth. 'I was at least an honest one before today.

Keeping quiet about your father makes me an accessory after the fact.'

'I'm sure your conscience can stand the strain!'

His gaze roved her face and hair, coming back to her mouth and staying there. 'I think it's going to have to,' he said on a fatalistic note. 'Some things a man just can't deny himself. I'll be waiting for you Monday night. Make it after seven.'

He had come to her in order to open the door, but he made no attempt to touch her. Only when she was in the lift dropping swiftly downwards did it occur to her that he hadn't even kissed her yet. No doubt he would make up for the ommission over the coming four weeks, if she went through with it. *If* she went through with it? She had to go through with it. He had given her no other choice.

# CHAPTER TWO

IT was almost six by the time she got back to the office, but both Carol and her father were still there waiting for her. In those few hours the latter had aged ten years, his face drawn with worry.

'I wanted to come after you,' he said, 'but Carol wouldn't let me.' His eyes searched hers, looking for some element of comfort. 'Thanks for trying. It can't have been pleasant.'

Lauren's smile felt stiff. 'It was productive though. He's going to hold off for a month to give you a chance to repay what you took.'

'He is!' The light brown eyes took on new life, his features relaxing into lines of sheer relief. 'Oh, God, I can't tell you how good that sounds! How on earth did you manage it?'

To Lauren that moment was worth everything she had gone through. She made a small, throwaway gesture. 'I appealed to his better nature. Can we go and eat? I don't suppose any of us had lunch.'

'My appetite has only just returned,' confessed her father. 'Give me a few minutes to clear my desk, and I'll take the two of you out to the best meal of your lives!'

'I need to tidy my hair,' announced Carol as he disappeared into the other office. 'Yours looks as if it could do with it too. Coming?'

Lauren followed her with some reluctance to the cloakroom down the corridor, too well aware that the other had not been so easily deceived. She was ready and waiting for the questioning glance turned on her the moment they were safely enclosed.

'So what really happened?' demanded Carol unequivocally. 'And don't try fobbing me off with that better nature story because I doubt if friend Brent has one!' She paused, viewing the vivid features before her with wry assessment. 'You paid a price, didn't you?'

Convincing her father was one thing, Lauren acknowledged ruefully; Carol was far too shrewd to believe anything but the truth.

'Not yet,' she said. 'I've even been offered a few weeks' holiday.'

'As what?'

'Ah, now that's the catch.' Lauren was trying to sound insouciant about it and not doing a bad job. 'My days may be spent alone but the nights will be a shared experience—or so I gathered. A travelling companion, he called it.'

'He can't do that!' Carol sounded shocked and distressed. 'Your father wouldn't let you go that far to save his skin!'

'Which is precisely why he mustn't ever know about it.' Lauren firmed her chin, green eyes determined. 'Promise me you won't tell him, Carol.'

'I can't. He has a right to know.'

'I don't care about his rights, only about keeping him out of jail!' Her voice softened. 'We both love him, we both know what it would do to him.'

'If it came to that.'

'It isn't a risk I'm prepared to take. Not when there's another way out.' She shrugged lightly. 'It could be a whole lot worse. A lot of girls would jump at the chance to be with Nick Brent in any capacity. After all, he's a very attractive man.'

Carol looked at her long and hard. 'Don't try making

out you don't really mind being forced to do this, Lauren. There's no way a woman could like a man of his kind!'

Liking had little to do with the way she felt about Nick Brent, Lauren was bound to allow. 'I don't intend he should enjoy it,' she said. 'With any luck, he'll be so bored with me he'll send me packing after a couple of days!'

'And turn Hugh in regardless?'

Lauren met her own eyes in the long mirror running above the washbasins, recalling the steely grey of another pair. 'Oddly enough, I think I do trust him to keep his word. He didn't ask for a certain performance standard.'

Carol said helplessly. 'What are you going to tell your father?'

'That's simple enough. I'll just say the job in Brussels was brought forward.'

'Do you think he'll believe it?'

'He won't have any reason to disbelieve it, providing you keep this to yourself.' Lauren gave a final flick with the comb and turned back to look at the woman in whom she was placing her trust. 'Whatever happens, I'll keep in touch.'

No weekend had ever seemed to pass with such grinding slowness. Lauren waited until Saturday evening to inform her father of the supposed change of plan.

'I heard yesterday,' she said, 'only it went out of my mind.'

'Hardly surprising,' Hugh Devlin agreed on a rueful note. 'It's a shame they didn't let you know sooner. You're barely going to have had any holiday between jobs at all!' He studied her for a moment, the hesitation only too apparent. 'Lauren, about yesterday when you went after Brent. He didn't . . . I mean you were gone so long.'

'He was the perfect gentleman,' she lied calmly. 'I had to wait until he got back from lunch, that's all.'

'Oh, I see.' He sounded relieved. 'I'd have stopped you going at all if I'd had any idea, but I have to confess to being thankful that you did. Not that he'll have any great respect for a man who allowed his daughter to plead his case. It must have been your future he was thinking of when he agreed to give me the time. Like your mother before you, you only have to smile at a man to have him like putty in your hands!'

That may have been true in her mother's day, Lauren thought dryly; it certainly didn't apply now. Nicholas Brent was a man of steel: cold and unbendable. The very thought of seeing him again sent tremors down her spine.

'You should marry Carol,' she declared out of the blue, surprising herself because she hadn't intended to bring that particular subject up. 'You could do a whole lot worse.'

'I know,' her father agreed. 'As a matter of fact, I've been thinking of doing just that for some time. You wouldn't mind?'

So she had been a relevant factor. Lauren wondered fleetingly where along the line she could have given the impression that she might object. 'Not one bit,' she assured him. 'Only don't make it too soon because I shan't be home for at least a month.'

He gave the first genuine smile of the day. 'You could always ask for compassionate leave. Don't worry, I have to get this mess cleared up and my self-respect back before I start asking any woman to share my life.'

That was an attitude Lauren could fully understand

and appreciate. Regaining her own self-respect was going to be no overnight affair.

Monday was a dull, wet day in tune with her spirits. The phone call at eleven caught her sitting huddled over a comforting mug of coffee in the kitchen of their Wimbledon home. The deep-timbred voice needed no introduction.

'Have you started packing yet?'

'What I'm going to need will hardly take long,' she responded coldly. 'I gather I'm to be there for your entertainment not my own.'

The smile came through in his tone. 'I think I can provide a fair comparison. Not to worry. What you don't have we can buy. Call it part of the deal.'

'I wouldn't take a penny piece from you!' Lauren clipped. 'You're not buying me, Mr Brent!'

'Blackmail was the word you used before, wasn't it?' He sounded amused. 'Have it your own way. There's been a slight change in plan, incidentally. I'll pick you up at ten-fifteen in the morning to go straight to the airport.'

The heaviness lifted a little. It was only a matter of a few hours, yet it felt like a reprieve. She would find some plausible reason to satisfy her father over the delay.

'I'll be ready,' she said, stifling the urge to try one more appeal to his better nature. She would only be wasting her time and her breath. The man was void of finer feeling. 'I just hope I can trust you, that's all.'

'Your father's safe enough.' The amusement had vanished. 'It's just you and me now. Ten-fifteen.'

Lauren put down the receiver slowly after he had rung off. Just you and me; there had been a threat in that statement. Planning a campaign of passive resistance was all very well, carrying it through something else again. Yet the thought of forcing herself to respond to his demands was more than she could bear. If only there was some escape!

Carol came home with her father for supper, the two of them expressing their surprise on finding Lauren still in residence.

'I got the dates mixed,' she said casually. 'It's tomorrow not today. 'I'm sorry if the two of you were counting on dining tête-à-tête.'

'We're going to have plenty of time to be alone together,' Hugh Devlin answered, smiling at the woman by his side. 'I asked Carol to marry me when this business is all over. She said yes.'

'What I actually said,' the latter put in, 'was that I saw no reason to wait that long, but your father won't agree.'

'Only because I daren't place too much reliance on Brent keeping his word,' came the wry response, 'and I don't want you tied to a jailbird.'

'He'll keep his word.' Lauren said it with as much conviction as she dared allow herself. 'Make it the last day of the month and I'll be there by hook or by crook!'

'It's a date.' Smiling, Hugh lifted his glass. 'To a long and honest future. You can bet your sweet life I shan't be tempted to make this kind of mistake again!'

Carol waited until she and Lauren were alone in the kitchen after the meal before asking the obvious question.

'So what really happened?'

'His choice not mine,' Lauren assured her. 'He's picking me up in the morning to fly to Rome. At least I'll be safe from the bottom pinchers.'

'Don't be flippant about it,' Carol remonstrated. 'It isn't funny.'

'I know.' Lauren gave her a straight and sober glance. 'But it's no use being miserable about it either. Dad's going to be okay. That's all that really matters.' She paused as a thought struck her. 'Assuming there's no chance he mightn't be able to repay the money after all! Just supposing this deal of his doesn't come off?'

'It will. It was the sheer "can't lose" aspect that provided the temptation in the first place.' Carol took up another of the delicate china plates and began carefully to dry it. 'Hugh is going to give the profit to charity.'

'All that risk for nothing. It hardly seems fair.'

'You're not suggesting he should keep it?'

Lauren smiled wryly and shook her head. 'Just a joke in bad taste. He may not be given a choice when it comes right down to it. Nick Brent could have other plans for any profit made.' Deliberately she lightened her tone. 'Anyway, let's forget that aspect for now. Are you planning a church wedding?'

'Registry office.' Carol's face had taken on a softer glow. 'If there's one good thing come out of all this it's that it made Hugh realise he needs someone.' She caught herself hastily up, glancing in Lauren's direction with a look of apology. 'Not that I'm denigrating your contribution. . . .'

'But a daughter can hardly supply the same degree of comfort as a wife,' Lauren finished for her. 'Don't worry, I'm not the jealous kind. I'm happy for you both.'

'Thanks, love.' The other paused and sighed. 'I only wish I could say the same about you.'

'I'll be fine.' Lauren wished she could feel as confident of that as she sounded. 'As I said before, he isn't going to find me all that interesting. Not compared with the kind of woman he's probably used to.'

There was a pause before Carol said slowly, 'Perhaps it's partly because he's bored with the kind of woman he is used to that he wants you with him. Not that I'm making excuses for him. There is no excuse for what he's doing! Lauren, there has to be another way. If you talked to him again. . . .'

'It wouldn't do any good.' That much Lauren could state with conviction. She rinsed the last cup and tipped the water from the bowl, forcing a lighter tone. 'There's a bright side to everything if one looks for it. I have never visited Rome. Not that I imagine we'll be spending the whole three weeks there.'

'I tried to check his itinerary,' Carol admitted. 'Only I didn't get very far. He likes to turn up unexpectedly in places.'

He would, thought Lauren caustically. Catch them on the hop! The smile was donned for the occasion. 'Well, there you are then—a mystery tour! Stop worrying about me. There are worse ways of seeing the world. Let's go and see what Dad's doing.'

There was no further opportunity to discuss the subject again that evening. Lauren took care of that. Only when she was finally alone in her own bedroom did she allow herself to contemplate what lay ahead. In about twenty-four hours from now she would be facing an experience against which all her sensibilities rebelled, yet she would let it happen because she must. Let being the operative word, she told herself with emphasis. It would be an odd kind of man who could gain any pleasure from a partner as totally unresponsive as she planned to be.

She was ready and waiting when the chauffeur-driven Daimler drew up outside the house the following morning. Hidden behind the living-room curtain, she watched Nick slide his lean length from the rear seat, resisting the impulse to dodge back as he glanced towards the house. He was wearing a dark suit of the same superb cut as the one he had worn on their previous meeting, his shirt a pristine grey and white stripe. There was something almost Italianate about those dark good looks of his, she decided as a stray breeze discovered a hint of curl in the thickness of his hair. Mixed parentage, perhaps—not that it was of any real interest.

She let him ring the bell three times before going to answer it, standing back in the hallway to allow him entrance without a word of greeting.

'My suitcase is still upstairs,' she said. 'I daresay you'll want to get your driver to fetch it.'

'No problem,' he returned easily. 'Just show me where.'

Lauren stayed where she was. 'First door on the right.'

'No . . .' his tone was still pleasant enough but the grey eyes had a glitter, 'I said show me.' He put a hand on her shoulder and turned her ahead of him, not exactly pushing yet not allowing any denial on her part either.

The bedroom door was closed. Lauren opened it and moved on into the room, indicating the suitcase at rest on the bed with a disdainful little sweep of her hand. 'There.'

She was disconcerted when he made no attempt to take it up, passing by the bed to throw open her wardrobe door and swiftly riffle through the clothing left hanging inside. The pale grey, hand-stitched jacket and toning skirt he selected she had herself deliberately passed over when choosing her travelling outfit. With unerring eye, he also picked out the silk shirt which went with the suit, holding out all three garments on their hangers towards her.

'You've got about five minutes to change,' he stated.

'Pride?' she taunted, and saw the firm lips thin.

'You could call it that, yes.' He put down the clothing on the bed when she failed to move, coming back to turn her forcefully to face the long cheval mirror a few feet away. 'Just take a good look at yourself, then tell me where yours got to.'

The reflection she saw was hardly a prepossessing one, Lauren was bound to admit. The dun-coloured dress she was wearing was one she had bought in a sale and subsequently pushed to the back of the wardrobe because it did absolutely nothing for her. With her hair scraped back from her face into the severe little bun and a total lack of make-up, she looked a wreck. She winced in spite of herself.

'We made a bargain,' he said softly. 'And this wasn't part of it!' He took the centre back neckline of the dress in both hands, ripping it down the seam with one swift tug then pushing the material forward so that it slid from her shoulders and halfway down her arms before she could stop it. 'I'll buy you a replacement when we get where we're going. And we *are* going. Make no mistake about it.'

Lauren nerved herself not to struggle as he pulled the retaining pins from her hair to let it drop heavily about her face, too conscious of the extreme brevity of the brassiere cupping the fullness of her breasts. She met his eyes through the mirror, found herself held by them, mesmerised by the penetrating steel of his gaze. The fingers still at her nape felt warm and strong; he rubbed the back of one of them gently against her skin, smiling as she tensed involuntarily to the movement.

'If we had the time,' he said, 'I'd claim a little of that compensation right now. Get dressed. I'll wait downstairs.'

Lauren waited until the door had closed behind him before letting the remains of the dress drop to the floor. Her skin tingled where his fingers had touched her. Just a nerve, she told herself: he had touched a nerve end, that was all. The detestation she felt was certainly in no way reduced by his actions. It burned in her like fire. It had been a forlorn hope that she might put him off the whole idea by appearing at her worst. All she had gained from that was the degradation of having her clothes literally ripped from her back. Nick Brent might appear the total gentleman on the surface, but underneath he was pure primitive, and nerve-shaking with it. It was going to take every ounce of guts she had to carry her through.

Dressed in the grey suit and silk shirt, it seemed ridiculous not to go the whole way and put on a touch of make-up. Nick had already taken her suitcase. He was standing in the hall by the front door when she went down. His nod signified approval.

'That's better. Let's go.'

The driver got out of the Daimler to take the suitcase and open the rear passenger door, his face beneath the navy uniform cap quite impassive.

'We're running late, sir,' he said. 'I might have to break a few speed limits.'

'Just do what's necessary,' came the smooth reply. 'I have to make that flight.' He glanced Lauren's way as he settled himself into the seat alongside her, mouth slanting. 'If I don't, I'll know who to blame. Hope you're prepared to pay the penalty.'

Lauren was glad of the glass partition cutting them off from the driver. What the latter's opinion of her presence on this trip might be she could only guess, but she doubted if she was far out. Nick had said this was the first time he had ever taken a woman with him; she wondered if that included secretaries. She had a feeling that the latter might very well be male anyway. A man like Nicholas Brent looked on women with too jaundiced an eye ever to make one privy to his business affairs.

'You're not going to give me the silent treatment all the way out, I hope,' he remarked as they got under way. 'If there's one thing I can't tolerate it's feminine sulks!'

'I don't sulk,' she said flatly without bothering to turn her head towards him. 'On the other hand, I don't see much point in conversation unless there's someone or something worth talking to or about. You don't qualify under either category, Mr Brent!'

'Make it Nick,' he advised, ignoring the insult. 'Formality's a mite out of place considering the way things are.'

'The way things are is purely your choice,' she reminded him, still gazing steadfastly out through the window. 'I'll stick to Mr Brent, if you don't mind.'

His laugh was short. 'You know, I can't make up my mind whether you're genuinely as dumb as you're making out to be, or plain bloody-minded. You're the one who started this, remember? "I'll do anything you want", isn't that what you said?'

That did bring her head round, though only so far. 'Yes, but. . . .'

'But nothing. I told you your father was safe, so stop carping about the price. The one-night stand you were offering hardly covered it.' He paused momentarily. 'What did you tell him, anyway?'

'I let him believe you were giving him a second chance out of the goodness of your heart,' she said with tart intonation. 'And he's only safe, as you put it, so long as he can repay the money he took, isn't he? From what I understand, there's only a faint chance of anything going wrong with this deal he made, but just supposing it does? He doesn't have the funds to put things right on his own, and you'd already have had payment in kind.'

He studied her narrowly. 'You're suggesting I should give you a personal guarantee that the account will be topped up in any event? I wonder if you're aware of the sum involved?'

Lauren hadn't thought her spirits could plunge any further, but they could and did. 'He said it was large,' she admitted.

Nick's laugh was humourless. 'It would certainly be one of the highest prices any man ever paid for a woman!' His gaze moved over her face, taking in the wide brow, the straight line of her nose, the ripeness of her mouth, dropping with inevitability down the slender column of her throat to the shadowed cleavage at the base of her open collar. 'I've a mind to turn you out right here and now,' he said softly, 'only it isn't my mind that's calling the tune. All right, you have my word.'

He hadn't actually said 'just make it worth my while' even if that's what he meant, Lauren consoled herself. Whether he would make that demand later remained to be seen. Whatever the sum involved, he could obviously well afford it. That fact alone salved any conscience she might have had.

They reached the airport five minutes before the final call for the flight, the last passengers to take their seats on the plane. Lauren had never previously flown first class. Belted into the deep comfort of the club chair with a solicitous steward hovering, she thought cynically that money had its advantages.

Drinks were on the house. The ginger-haired steward

served up her order of coke without a flicker of an eyebrow.

'Proving something?' asked Nick on a low note of amusement as the man moved on. 'You can't really like that stuff!'

'I like it a whole lot better than the stuff you're drinking,' she responded with a derogatory glance at the whisky glass in front of him. 'I don't have to run true to type, do I?'

'You haven't done that since the day I met you,' he admitted. 'Strange, but when I saw you standing there in the office I'd have sworn butter wouldn't melt in your mouth. It just goes to show how deceptive appearances can be.'

'Not always.' Her tone held deliberation. 'I had you down for a complete louse from the word go!'

One lean hand came out to cover hers where it rested on her knee, fingers closing with just a hint of the strength behind them. 'Don't take too many liberties,' he advised softly. 'Tolerance isn't my strong point.'

She refrained from any attempt to pull the hand away, letting it lie limply under his. 'You say that as if you might be proud of the fact.'

'I was stating plain and simple fact,' he responded. 'Maybe I should practise more.

Lauren was silent for a long moment, desperate to be rid of his touch. She stiffened when he lifted the hand he held and turned it over into his palm, fingers curling as if in defence against his inspection.

'This new job you're due to start,' he said unexpectedly. 'What is it?'

'Office cleaner,' she retorted, and saw his lips widen briefly.

'In other words, none of my business. All right, I'll accept that. What you do with your life is your own affair. All I ask is a few weeks of your undivided attention.'

Lauren said shortly, 'You mean demand.'

'If you like.' He released her, putting his head back against the rest and closing his eyes with an air of dismissal.

Lauren concentrated her own attention on the white carpet of cloud below, thinking of the everyday, ordinary things she would have been doing had this never happened; of the plans she had made to cover the coming weeks. She was due in Brussels on the first of the month. Nick had said they would be back in England by the twenty-eighth, which would leave her with just three clear days in which to settle all her affairs. Not that it was really going to take so much doing. Her papers were in order, and accommodation organised. All she had left was to sort out her personal belongings, and not even that with any kind of finality because she would be coming home at fairly regular intervals.

The real problem was that she didn't want to go at all, she acknowledged for the first time. She had been earning enough in her last job to afford a small flat, which would have served the same purpose so far as her father and Carol were concerned, and at least left her within reach of familiar haunts. By the time she got back from this present jaunt she would have had her fill of foreign climes.

Nick's head was still back when she glanced round at him, his eyes still closed. She studied the chiselled profile, following the taut stretch of tanned skin over high cheekbones, the smooth line of his jaw; dwelling for a timeless period on the shape of his mouth in relaxation. One arm lay along the rest between them, his hand curved over the edge. A good hand, long and fleshless, the tendons clearly visible beneath the skin. She imagined that same hand exploring her body, feeling the tremor start deep within her. He would know exactly where and how to elicit reaction, but response was something else again. No matter what he did to her she would lie there like the proverbial log. Detesting him the way she did it shouldn't be difficult.

'I'm no different from any other man,' he said softly and unexpectedly, still without opening his eyes. 'You'd already got that settled in your mind before you came to see me the other day. If it's right that familiarity breeds contempt, this can hardly be the first time you've sung for your supper, so why not resign yourself to the inevitable?'

'Supposing I told you I was a virgin?' Lauren responded on a low taut note, and saw his mouth tilt sardonically as his head turned towards her. His eyes held derision.

'You can tell me anything you like.'

She held his gaze for just a few brief seconds before looking away again, incapable of sustaining that much control. A part of her wanted to revert to childhood: to beat at him with clenched fists and scream insulting names. What on earth had possessed her to say that? She could have anticipated his reaction. He was right about one thing though: she did regard most things male with contempt. This face and body of hers might be Nature's gifts, but they provided an image totally at variance with her inner needs.

It was raining when they landed. Greeted by name when they went through passport control, Nick replied to the man in fluent Italian, laughing at some remark Lauren made no attempt to interpret.

'I'm going to send you on ahead with the bags and let you check into the hotel,' he stated at the taxi rank outside. 'I've an appointment in less than half an hour. Just give the desk clerk my name. The suite is ready booked. Anything you want, you can order through room service. I'll be there around five.'

Lauren got into the vehicle and sat back in the seat without answering. Nick closed the door and paid the driver. The last she saw of him was a tall figure stepping back as the taxi pulled away. It was good to be alone again, even if only for a little while. By the time Nick rejoined her she had to be in total command of herself. Only that way could she hope to come out on top.

# CHAPTER THREE

MIRACULOUSLY, the clouds lifted and vanished during the journey from the airport. Lauren gazed fascinated from the window of the taxi-cab at a passing scene so steeped in history one half expected to see ranks of Legionnaires marching the streets. The city was packed with tourists, cameras at the ready, heads turning this way and that. There was noise and heat, a thousand different odours mingled on the air. Lauren felt stimulated, seized by the senses. For a while she even managed to forget the real reason she was here in the Eternal City.

The hotel was old, set in a large square, its interior decor all gilt and crystal and silk-screened walls. The name of Brent elicited immediate recognition on the part of the young male receptionist. He even had her own name on mental file. Lauren registered the bold appraisement in his eyes without allowing her gaze to flinch. It didn't matter what other people thought of the relationship between her and Nick. They would not be the only unmarried couple staying together in the hotel by a long chalk!

She could feel him watching her as she crossed the lobby in the wake of the porter assigned to carry her bags, and was glad when the lift doors closed. Acting blasé about the whole affair was one thing, actually feeling it quite another. Nick had a devil of a nerve leaving her to check in here alone, yet if she were honest with herself she had to admit that his presence could have made things even worse. She had a couple of hours now in which to gather her resources. She was going to need every moment.

The suite was luxurious, consisting of a large and comfortably furnished sitting room with separate bedroom and bath. Lauren viewed the six-foot wide, satin-quilted bed with heavy heart. Two divans would at least have provided some kind of privacy, even if only after the event.

Thinking about the night to come brought a feeling close to panic. She couldn't go through with it. Not this way! If she left now was Nick really likely to turn her father in? His reasons for not doing so at once were hardly creditable. Certainly his co-directors were unlikely to share his point of view.

She knew she daren't take the risk. Nick was clever. He would have covered himself. She was stuck with the situation and had better make the best of it, any way she could.

Unpacking took only a few minutes considering what little she had brought. Nick's leather suitcase she left strictly alone. Even if he had provided her with keys, she would not have been prepared to perform that particular service for him.

Changed from the grey suit into a simple blue cotton dress, she found herself with still more than an hour to go before his arrival. He would expect her to stay put in the suite, she was pretty sure, but there was no way she could bring herself to do it. A walk would clear her head if nothing else.

The same young man was still on duty at the desk when she went down. He smiled at her with familiarity, eyes travelling the length of her body as she walked from the lift. Lauren was too far away to catch the remark he made to his fellow receptionist, and in all likelihood would not have understood the words anyway, but there was no mistaking the swift grin which crossed the other's face. She passed the desk without turning her head, knowing her colour was high.

The air outside was hot and humid after the rain, the square thronged with traffic and pedestrians. Lauren took a right turn into the Via Claudia, delighted to see the bulk of the Colosseum looming but a short distance ahead. If nothing else, she could fulfil a few personal ambitions while she was here.

A girl on her own in Rome was a natural target for the Italian male of any age, she discovered before she had covered more than a few hundred yards. One needed no understanding of the language to interpret the calls, the whistles, the ribald invitations. One youth kept pace with her on a motor scooter, dark eyes boldly appraising as he extended an obvious invitation to take a seat behind him on the pillion.

'Americano?' he asked when she failed to respond. 'I show you a good time!'

She shook him off eventually at the entrance to the Colosseum, although he made no immediate attempt to drive away, running the scooter in a small, idling circle as if he had every intention of staying there until she emerged again. With so many people coming and going, it shouldn't be too difficult to dodge him, Lauren told herself, hoping she was right. The young man's persistence was wearing, especially as she lacked the words to tell him what she really thought. An Italian phrase book was hardly likely to contain the kind of invective she needed to get her message across either, she acknowledged in wry amusement, eyeing the choice of several on the stand before her. She bought a guide instead, paying in sterling without bothering to check the rate of exchange. Nick had offered her lira on the plane coming over, but she had refused to take it. She had her Euro card with her should the need arise. In the meantime she would manage.

Despite the thronging crowds, the vast, crumbling ellipse of masonry cast its timeless spell. Lauren set out to climb to the topmost terrace, looking out through the embrasures at the hills, the Forum far below, the wide boulevards with their teeming traffic made toylike by distance. Up here there was hardly any sound. One could sit in the sunshine and imagine an age long gone. Lauren leaned her head against the warm stone and closed her eyes, forgetful for the moment of anything but just being here.

'Fantastic, isn't it?' commented a male voice in English. 'First time for you too?'

Reluctantly, Lauren turned her head to look at the fair-haired young man in jeans and T-shirt standing at the next embrasure along, returning his friendly smile. 'Yes, it is—to both questions.'

Encouraged, he moved to join her, resting an elbow on the crumbling parapet to look out over the city. 'I've wanted to come to Rome for years, but never got round to it before. It gets to you, doesn't it?' He turned his gaze back to her, eyes frankly admiring. 'Are you on your own?'

'For the moment,' she acknowledged, trying not to think too far ahead. 'And you?'

'The same. I was supposed to share this package tour with a friend, but she had family problems. I'm Gerry Reynolds, by the way.'

'Lauren Devlin,' she acknowledged resignedly.

'Lauren? That's unusual. Suits you though.' The pause begged more information. 'Are you here on holiday yourself?' he prompted when she made no attempt to provide it.

'Yes.' It was far from the truth but the only reasonable answer she could give.

'You're staying in Rome?'

'Only for a couple of days,' she said, not at all certain even of that much.

'You mean you're travelling.' He looked disappointed. 'Where's your next stop?'

'I'm not really sure,' Lauren admitted, already regretting letting herself in for this in the first place. 'Where the fancy takes me, I expect.'

'It's a good way to go—for some.' The tone was halfway between approval and censure. 'You've a lot of guts moving around on your own—especially the way you look! Had any trouble yet?'

Lauren forced a smile. 'Nothing I can't handle.'

'You've been lucky then. You need to watch out for these Italians. They don't take no for an answer by all accounts.' The hesitation was brief. 'Do you fancy a coffee or something?'

'That would have been nice,' she said, 'but I'm afraid I have to go. I'm meeting someone at five.'

Gerry looked at his watch. 'It's almost that already.' He made a wry little gesture as she got to her feet. 'Thanks for the company anyway.'

'Thank you for the offer.' She was moving away as she spoke, half turning to smile back at him. 'I hope you enjoy the rest of your stay.'

Lonely or not, he stood a better chance of that than she did, came the dry reflection as she descended the steps. Nick had said he would be at the hotel around five. What he might do if he arrived before her was anyone's guess. Yet he could hardly imagine she had taken off, could he, when her baggage was still there?

It was five-twenty by the time she gained the hotel. The lobby area was awash with people both coming and going. She had several minutes to wait for a lift, which stopped at every floor on its way back up. The suite was on the fourth, at the end of a short corridor. Lauren opened the door with the key she had not bothered to turn into reception on her departure, stepping through to the inner lobby and the man standing waiting for her in the sitting-room doorway opposite.

'Reception phoned through to say you were on your way up,' he stated curtly. 'Where the hell have you been?'

'Out,' she said, closing the door behind her with a sense of cutting off her last escape route. 'I needed some air.'

'Till this time? I'm told you left the hotel within minutes of getting here.'

Her 'friend' on the desk, Lauren surmised. 'I didn't realise I was to be confined to quarters,' she retorted. 'It wasn't part of the deal.'

'But this was.' Eyes hard, he came over, pulling her to him. His mouth was ruthless, brushing aside her involuntary protest. Lauren forced herself to stand still in his grasp, lips cold as her heart. She made no move even when he slid one hand down to find her breast through the thin material of her dress, hating his touch yet conscious of a tautening of muscle deep down at the very pit of her stomach.

She put up a nerveless hand the moment he let her go and deliberately wiped the back of it across her lips. 'Finished?' she asked with scorn.

'Not by a long chalk.' The anger had vanished, control restored. 'We've a long way to go, you and I, but I can wait.'

Lauren stayed where she was for a moment or two after he had gone back into the sitting room, uncertain of her next move. Her mouth felt tender, her lips slightly swollen from the pressure applied. Wait till when? she wondered.

'There's coffee and sandwiches through here,' he called unexpectedly. 'It's going to be several hours before you get another chance to eat.'

She went through the door slowly, aware of confusion. He had poured two cups, and had taken his own to a seat on one of the ornate sofas, leaving hers on the trolley. The sandwiches were concealed beneath a huge starched napkin. For the first time she realised just how hungry she was.

Nick watched her take cup and plate to a seat as far away from him as possible, mouth tilted sardonically.

'We're going to the home of a business acquaintance,' he announced. 'It's a rather special party, so you'll need to dress for the occasion. Did you bring anything suitable?'

Lauren met his gaze with all the equability she could muster. 'I doubt it.'

'I doubted it too,' he agreed, looking anything but perturbed, 'so I took the liberty of stopping off to buy you the necessary items. They're in the bedroom.'

'I'm no Barbie Doll,' she countered. 'Supposing I choose not to wear them?'

His expression didn't alter. 'You'll wear them,' was all he said.

'Even if they're not the right size—or are you such an expert when it comes to guessing?'

'Pretty fair,' came the unmoved reply. 'I didn't get a good look at your feet so I brought several pairs of sandals. The ones you don't wear can be returned.'

'You think of everything,' Lauren said with sarcasm, and received a mocking inclination of the dark head.

'I try.' He studied her for a moment, head still tilted slightly to one side, eyes taking on a deeper glint. His hand was perfectly steady as he reached out to put down his cup. 'I don't think I want to wait any longer,' he said. 'We have the time.'

It had to happen sooner or later, Lauren told herself heavily, so why not now? The sooner he realised she was not what he imagined she was the better. Once might even be enough for him.

This time there was no need for his guiding hand at her back. She moved ahead of him like an automaton to the bedroom, amazed at her own lack of emotion. At the side of the bed itself she slid off her sandals and turned back the silk cover before lying down on her back to gaze unseeingly at the ornate plaster ceiling.

'I'm ready,' she said.

'For what?' Nick sounded amused. 'I don't mind doing the undressing, but I'm going to have trouble getting that dress off while you're lying down—unless you want me to do some more tearing.' He sat down on the side of the bed and took her chin in one strong hand, forcing her to look at him. 'Some women enjoy a little roughing up. Is that your particular bent?'

'No.' Her tone was wooden. 'The agreement was that I came with you and made myself available. That's exactly what I'm doing.'

'Oh, I see. A kind of passive resistance?' The sudden gleam in his eyes was unnerving. 'I always did like a challenge!'

Lauren made herself totally limp as he rolled her over to get at the long back zip of her dress. He rolled her again to pull the material down from her shoulders and over her hips, easing the garment off via her legs and feet and dropping it carelessly on the floor. Under it she was wearing nothing but a scanty lace bra and briefs, but he made no immediate attempt to remove those too, taking his time in studying her body.

'Beautiful,' he said. 'Smooth-skinned, long-legged and a waist I could almost span with both hands! You've been given an unfair advantage over the rest of your sex, Lauren. With that face of yours and this body you have it made. But you already know that, don't you? This isn't the first time you've used your assets to get what you want. Not that I'm denigrating your filial devotion in this particular case. It's highly commendable.'

'Just get on with it!' she gritted between her teeth, and saw him smile.

'If I did just that you wouldn't like it. Neither would I. We'll start slow and build up to it—this way.'

She kept her eyes open and fixed as he bent to put his lips to hers, feeling the cool silky texture of his shirt against her bare skin. His mouth pressured hers apart, the tip of his tongue finding its way inside to rim the very edges of her teeth with a lightness of touch that had every nerve ending in her body tensing in unison.

His hands were at her waist, spanning it the way he had described, his fingers almost but not quite touching across the arch of her spine. Then they were moving again, sliding with infinite slowness down to the lacy top of her briefs, pausing there for a heart-stopping moment before continuing on over the material to cup the curve of her buttocks and gently caress.

Staying inviolate to that onslaught of sensation took all of Lauren's willpower. She wanted to move to his urging, to feel those hands of his all over her body. When he came on top of her she could feel his weight and hardness bearing her down, spreading her thighs to accommodate him. Nothing she had experienced before had prepared her for this degree of involuntary response. She had to stiffen herself both mentally and physically in order to survive.

'You don't intend making this easy, do you?' he murmured against her lips. 'That suits me too. I'm going to enjoy getting through to you, Lauren. Before we've finished you'll be begging me to make love to you!'

'Never!' she breathed, and he laughed softly.

'Never's a long time. You may hate me because I insisted on full payment when you hoped to get away with less, but you're too sensual a female to hold out against your own instincts. We'll make a rare union when it happens. One worth waiting a little longer for, I think.' He pushed himself suddenly upright so that he was sitting astride her, pressing down on her hips so that she couldn't move the lower half of her body and smiling at the fire in her eyes. 'Tonight we'll have no restrictions between us—of any kind. I might even be able to teach you a few tricks you don't already know. I'll certainly do my best.' He slid off her and stood up, turning towards the bathroom. 'I need a cold shower right now.'

I hope you drown in it! Lauren thought, but refrained from voicing the sentiment.

It was several moments before she could stir herself to get off the bed. There were several boxes of varying sizes lying on the chaise longue. The thought of damaging the garments contained within beyond repair fleetingly crossed her mind, but that would be a futile gesture when he could so easily obtain more. If she were totally honest with herself, she was also just a little afraid of his possible reaction to such a wanton act. He had few scruples. He had already proved that much.

The sandals he had spoken of turned out to be flimsy scraps of gold leather. The second pair she tried fitted her perfectly: she could scarcely feel them on her feet. Another box contained several pairs of finest stockings of the kind which stayed up on their own through the built-in garter at the top, along with pure silk briefs so miniscule they were no more than two triangles of material held together with a ribbon thread at each hip. She had been right about Nick being a sensualist, Lauren thought grimly, but he was going to be disappointed if he imagined she would wear *these* for him!

It was only when she took the dress from its box and held it up against her in front of the long dressing mirror that she realised why the matching undergarment had to be so scanty. She stared at it for several cold-eyed seconds before folding it carefully back into its tissue. No way, she told herself furiously. Not for anyone or anything!

She was sitting in a chair waiting when Nick came out from the bathroom. He was wearing a smallish towel knotted about his waist and nothing else.

'It's all yours,' he said, crossing to the wardrobes on the far wall. 'Don't take all night.'

'If you wanted a call girl to take to your precious party,' Lauren said through her teeth, 'why didn't you send for a real one!'

'Call girls don't perform that particular service,' he returned without turning round. 'Anyway, I doubt if I'd find one to look the way you're going to look tonight.'

'I won't wear it,' she said desperately. 'And you can't make me!'

He turned then, shirt slung casually over a bare shoulder. His eyes were hard. 'I can and you will,' he stated. 'If you've any doubts on that score, I'll put you into it myself!'

'Why?' she demanded. 'Why that dress?'

'Because I want you to be the focus of attention.'

'Why?' she asked again, but he shook his head.

'You'll know when the time comes.' The pause was brief, his expression unrelenting. 'Are you going to get ready, or shall I put through a call regarding a certain account?'

Lauren bit her lip. 'You really do use every low weapon you can lay your hands on, don't you?'

'It depends on the circumstances,' he said. 'Right now I'll use whatever's necessary.'

'Including force?'

'No, I changed my mind about that. We might tear the dress. It's an exclusive.'

'It would have to be.' She waited another moment, knowing even as she did so that it was useless expecting any softening on his part. He was ruthless enough to carry out his threat. In the end there was nothing else for it but to obey.

With the door safely if somewhat immaterially locked between them, Lauren took a quick shower and made up her face. The briefs and gossamer fine stockings were almost exactly the colour of her flesh, the dress itself a shimmer of gold, fitting like a second skin from shoulder to ankle, with walking made possible only by the split seam to just above knee level at the left side. There was no brassiere because it would have been impossible to design one that would not have been seen beneath the plunging V of the neckline, the latter cut to reveal the thrusting inner sides of both breasts whilst barely covering her nipples. Lauren felt naked. It took all of her nerve to unlock the door and emerge from the bathroom to meet Nick's scrutiny.

He was already dressed in a white tuxedo and dark trousers, a black cummerbund swathing his waist. A low whistle escaped his lips as he looked at her standing there.

'Even better than I imagined,' he said. 'It takes a rare figure to wear something like that.'

'It takes a rare kind of mind to dream it up,' she responded bitterly. 'I might just as well be nude!'

His smile taunted her. 'Nudity leaves nothing to the imagination.'

'You think this does?'

'Enough.' He bent and opened a long narrow case on the bedside table and took out something that glinted gold, coming over to where she stood. 'Turn around and lift up your hair at the back.'

Lauren did so, to find herself facing one of the mirrored wardrobe doors. She willed herself to keep perfectly still as he clasped the thin gold chain behind her neck, feeling the heaviness of the single mounted pearl nestling between her breasts.

'Just the bracelet,' he said, 'and that's perfect. This lily needs little gilding.'

She fastened the narrow gold band about her own wrist, looking up when she had finished to meet his gaze through the mirror. The high heels she was wearing brought the top of her head on a level with his nose, so that his eyes were all she could see. He was standing so close she could feel the heat from his body. When he slid both hands under her arms to cover her breasts she made no move to stop him, allowing the curl of her lip to convey its own message.

'Later,' he promised, caressing her. 'You'll feel differently then.'

Her body was reacting right now to that intimate touch, and there was nothing she could do to stop it. Dismayed, she watched her nipples peak beneath the thin material, felt the tensing of her thighs against the sudden stirring of sensation. Physically it was going to be too easy; she knew that now. He could rouse her regardless. Strength of mind was what she needed. She could only hope she was going to be capable of summoning it when the time came.

# CHAPTER FOUR

ROME by night was an experience Lauren would have preferred to enjoy alone. Nick spoke little during the drive across the city, gazing out of his own window as if wrapped in thought. She wondered once if he might be regretting the situation as much as she did, but decided it was unlikely. There was no room in this man's life for regrets.

Their destination lay across the river outside the inner city boundaries: a large house of modern design set within floodlit grounds. Arriving vehicles formed a line to deposit their passengers at the foot of a curve of steps. Helped from her seat by Nick's firm guiding hand, Lauren steeled herself to mount the imposing flight at his side, to ignore, or try to ignore, the steady pressure of his hand beneath her elbow.

Wide doors stood open to the night, allowing a stream of light to flood the area. They followed a couple who appeared to be arguing about something, although with little understanding of the language, Lauren could not be sure she was right about that. Italians were volatile by nature. Even their ordinary, everyday speech sounded fast and furious by her standards.

A manservant took her gold cloth cloak at the door, leaving her defenceless before the suddenly arrested gazes of every male within sight. Head held high, she moved alongside Nick down the length of the fine hallway to an inner door where their host and hostess were receiving guests.

Several other people were ahead of them. Beyond, Lauren could see through to a huge, brightly lit room already thronged. Most of the men wore white tuxedos, with just one or two in the traditional black and white, but it was the women who took the eye with their gorgeous and glamorous creations. She was not alone in revealing a lot of flesh, she was thankful to note, although no neckline that she could see from where she stood plunged quite so low as her own.

It was their turn now to be greeted. Nick was murmuring introductions, but the names barely registered. The couple were in their mid to late forties, the man a typical Latin with his smooth black hair, olive skin and bold eyes—the latter fastening on Lauren's décolleté with unconcealed lust as he bent his lips to the back of her hand. His wife said something to Nick that brought a faint smile to his lips.

'*Si*,' he agreed.

More people were arriving behind them. With reluctance, their host released Lauren's hand and turned to do his duty. Heads turned as the two of them progressed further into the room. Whispered comments reached Lauren's ears. She kept her poise by sheer effort of will, refusing to resort to the fixed smile of the socially ill-at-ease. As if by magic a path slowly opened up ahead of them as they moved, guiding their footsteps in one direction. Nick took two glasses of bubbling champagne from a tray carried by a passing waiter, handing one over to her with a quizzical lift of one dark brow.

'Keep it up,' he murmured. 'You're doing just fine!'

Lauren would have liked to toss the champagne straight into the handsome face, but self-preservation was the stronger emotion even then. She allowed herself one sip from the glass to calm her nerves, surprised to find her hand perfectly steady. Either she was a better actress than she had ever given herself credit for, or too numb from the strain to react. It scarcely mattered which at the moment. Just providing she could get through the rest of this evening with the same kind of aplomb.

The couple right up ahead of them had not moved like the others, the female of the two standing with her back turned in their direction as she listened to whatever it was her companion was saying to her. A long and lovely back, Lauren could see, its skin a smooth, unblemished olive right down to the very apex of the spinal column which the emerald green material so barely skimmed before lifting to the swell of two perfect hemispheres. Her hair was black as jet, combed back and up from the nape of her neck into an emerald-studded comb.

It was the man who saw them coming, his whole face undergoing a swift change of expression. He said one word, swift and sharp to the woman in front of him, eliciting a faint stiffening of the naked back. Then she was turning, and Lauren found herself looking at one of the most beautiful faces she had ever seen, the eyes huge and dark and somehow expectant, the mouth a full red invitation. Seen from the front, the emerald green dress defied gravity, suspended only by the perfect cut and fit of the shaped bodice.

'Nicholas?' she said softly, then her eyes fell on Lauren and the smile faded, a glitter springing alive in the dark depths of her gaze.

'Lauren Devlin—Francesca and Luigi Bardini,' supplied Nick. There was a faint note of malice in his tone. He continued to speak in English, whether for her benefit or some reason of his own, Lauren couldn't be sure. 'Congratulations, the two of you. I'm only sorry I couldn't make the wedding.' The pause was brief but meaningful. 'I hope you'll both be very happy.'

The other man looked small and swarthy in comparison with Nick's long, lean length. He was also, Lauren noted, at least twenty years older than his bride. There was an air of possessiveness in the way he rested his hand along the shapely bare arm, a certain challenge in the lift of his greying head. 'We will,' he said with assurance, and also in English. 'With me, Francesca will want for nothing!'

She was wanting for something right now, thought Lauren, watching the changing expression in the dark eyes as the Italian woman looked at Nick. There was pain hidden deep in there. Then she laughed and the impression was gone, replaced by a malice of her own.

'Nothing,' she agreed in husky accents. 'Luigi satisfies my every need!'

Those in close proximity to their little group were listening avidly to the exchange. Lauren was thankful when Nick took her arm to move her on away from the other couple, copying his polite little smile of farewell.

'You dressed me up like a dog's dinner just for that!' she said on a low and bitter note as he stopped to exchange her half-empty glass for a fresh one from one of the many trays held by the waiters circulating the room. 'Why?'

'To show that there are other women in the world equally desirable,' Nick returned flatly. 'She married Luigi to teach me a lesson. Well, now I've taught her one.'

'She was your mistress?' Lauren hazarded, and felt his sharp glance.

'If you can guess so much why not fill in the rest?'

'All right, I will.' She kept her voice quiet the way he was doing so that they appeared to be carrying on a normal conversation to anyone still watching them. 'She wanted marriage and you didn't, but your pride suffered when she chose it in preference to you. You'd naturally want to have your cake and eat it too!'

'Naturally.' His tone was smooth, but the anger wasn't far away. 'A man doesn't marry a woman like Francesca.'

'Luigi did.'

'Because he's a fool. He believes he can alter basic nature.'

Lauren looked back at him steadily. 'Perhaps he can. You wouldn't know anything about the power of love, would you? I doubt if you ever loved anyone in your life!'

The handsome face was a mask. 'If you're talking of women, then you're quite right. I never found one I could trust for long enough.'

'Only because you haven't looked in the right places.'

'So tell me where they are,' he challenged. 'Show me one female who isn't prepared to utilise every asset she has to her own ends and I'll marry her tomorrow!'

'Always providing a nice girl like that would want to marry a man like you,' Lauren came back acidly. 'She'd want tenderness, to start with, and that's an emotion you couldn't even begin to understand.'

'And you would?' He was controlling himself with an effort, the skin taut about his mouth. 'You and Francesca are two of a kind.'

'Except that I'm with you for my father's sake not my own.'

'Are you so sure of that?' The hard jeering edge was designed to penetrate. 'Having a father in jail would hardly have enhanced your prospects. You could even have lost the job in Brussels through it.'

Lauren was silent for a long moment, staring at him

with slightly widened eyes. 'How did you know about that?' she got out at last.

'I took the trouble to make inquiries. It wasn't difficult.'

'Then why bother asking me on the plane this morning?'

Broad shoulders lifted in a shrug. 'Why indeed? Perhaps I had a faint hope of a straight answer. Only you'd no intention of letting your motives seem anything but purely altruistic, had you?'

Pride would allow her no denial. 'If you want to see it that way.'

People were beginning to look at the two of them again, sensing the conflict if not actually understanding it. Nick reached out and took her glass, depositing it along with his own on the nearest surface. 'There's dancing in the other room,' he stated. 'We'll give it another half an hour before we leave.'

It was still barely nine now. The thought of what was to be faced when they returned to the hotel room made Lauren bite her lip. 'You don't mind people guessing that you only put in an appearance at all for one reason?' she asked slyly as he drew her with him towards the sound of music.

'They don't have to guess,' came the prompt reply. 'They've already seen the reason—or as much of her as I intend to allow.' His smile mocked. 'When we leave early they'll know the reason for that too—at least the men certainly will. There'll be many who'd gladly change places with me tonight.'

'Except Luigi,' she said daringly, and felt his fingers tighten under her elbow.

'Don't try getting at me that way. So far as I'm concerned, Francesca is a closed book.'

The space allocated for dancing was limited. Of

necessity Nick was forced to hold her close, his hand warm in the centre of her back. She could feel the strength of his thighs against hers as they moved, the quivering of sensation at the centre of her body. If just being close to him like this affected her in such a way, what would it be like later when he was really trying? she wondered desperately. How far could strength of mind take precedence? Hate him she might, but he was still the most devastating male she had ever met—and he knew exactly what he was doing to her.

'Am I allowed to ask you any personal questions?' she murmured eventually just to break the silence between them.

'Depends on what they are,' he returned. 'Try me.'

She waited a moment before doing so. 'It's just that I wondered if you had any Italian blood yourself. You speak the language so fluently, and you have a certain look about you.'

'My mother was Italian,' he acknowledged. 'I was brought up to be bi-lingual, despite my father's preferences.'

'He objected?'

'Isn't that what I just said?' Nick sounded derisive. 'He married my mother against her family's wishes—in fact, they refused to recognise the marriage initially. Can you blame him for preferring to turn his back on them?'

'I'd have said your mother had more cause to be bitter,' Lauren responded. 'She must have loved him very much.'

'So much that she left him to return to Italy when I was eight years old.'

Lauren drew back her head a little in order to see his face, momentarily forgetting who and what he was in the swiftness of her sympathy. 'Leaving you behind?'

'No, she took me with her.'

Her brows drew together. 'Then you grew up right here in this country?'

'Only until my father won his case for custody. I was a British subject.' The grey eyes had little expression. 'I suppose he thought if he had me she might come back to him.'

'But she didn't?'

'No, she didn't. I spent years being shuttled back and forth between the two of them instead.'

'Not wholly your mother's fault,' Lauren pointed out midly. 'Yet you obviously only blame her.'

'She isn't the one I. . . .' He broke off with a sudden impatient movement. 'It's immaterial now. She's been dead seven years.'

'And your father?'

'Three.' The jeering little smile was back. 'So you see, I've no one to think about but myself.'

'A fact you take full advantage of.'

'Quite.' His glance roved her face and hair, coming back to meet her eyes without any hint of softening. 'I think we're ready to go.'

'We haven't eaten yet,' Lauren reminded him, playing for time. 'You only allowed me half a sandwich.'

'And now you're fading away from hunger.' He gave a mock sigh. 'Never let it be said I took a woman to bed on an empty stomach!'

Lauren found herself led from the floor and deposited on an ornate gilt-and-brocade sofa. 'Stay put,' Nick ordered. 'I'll bring you a plate back here.'

She watched him go, threading his way between the various groups of people with a word here and there. Half Italian, yet the Latin temperament revealed itself only in minor ways. He was so much the man in command—as hard as nails. She wondered what it would take to get through to him.

'The lovely English rose has been deserted?' asked a heavily accented male voice some few moments later, and Lauren turned her head to look into a pair of dark eyes filled with the kind of appraisement becoming all too familiar. The man was older than Nick by a dozen years, his features thickened yet not unattractive in a coarse kind of way. A diamond ring flashed on one little finger as he lifted a seemingly negligent hand to touch the petals of the flower in his buttonhole, the stone many-faceted and almost blue in colour. As a declaration of worth, Lauren thought cynically, it left little unsaid.

'He'll be back,' she answered. 'He went to find some food.'

'Ah, now that is a pity—although I should know better than to hope for such good fortune.' He paused delicately. 'You have been for very long with Signor Brent?'

'We only arrived in Rome today,' she said, purposely misunderstanding the nuances of the question. 'I'm sorry, I didn't catch your name, signor.'

'Macchioni,' he supplied. 'Marcello Macchioni.' His eyes moved with slow deliberation down the length of her throat to the thrusting V of her breasts, lingering there quite openly. 'Anyone,' he added, 'will tell you I am the most generous of men. Should you choose to leave your protector. . . .'

He left the rest unspoken, but with no doubt as to his meaning. Lauren clamped down hard on her first instinctive reaction. Telling this man what she thought of his generous offer would be a total waste of time and breath. He probably wouldn't even understand her anger. So far as anyone here was concerned, she was

Nicholas Brent's new mistress—replacement for the one who had deserted him. Nick himself had done everything to foster that image.

He was coming back now, two heaped plates of food held high as he moved through the crowd. Without haste, her new admirer moved off, apparently too well aware that his name alone would be all she needed should she feel inclined to make the change. The dress she was wearing was as much responsible for his attitude as anything, Lauren acknowledged. No woman of class would choose it for herself. A man doesn't marry a woman like Francesca, Nick had said—a statement which had included her too. Not that she would want to marry a man like Nick anyway. God help the woman who did!

'What was Macchioni saying to you,' he demanded as he handed over one of the loaded plates. 'As if I couldn't guess!'

'If you can guess there isn't much point in my telling you,' Lauren rejoined equably.

'But you'll do it anyway.' He sat down beside her, expression daring her to defy him. 'Word for word.'

'Word for word I don't remember,' she said, 'but he seemed convinced he could make me a more attractive offer.' She lifted a pair of defiantly sparkling green eyes. 'Of the two of you, he was at least open in his intentions!'

Nick lifted a sardonic brow. 'You're saying I haven't been?'

'Not wholly, no. You gave me no idea you intended parading me like some piece of merchandise you just went out and bought! You knew you were going to bring me here tonight before ever you gave me that ultimatum, didn't you? That telephone call in your apartment the other afternoon was from Rome.'

'Considering you heard me speaking Italian, that might be a fair assumption.' He studied her a moment as if waiting for something more, shrugging when she tightened her lips. 'So I brought you with me for more than one purpose. Would it have made any difference to our arrangement if you'd known that?'

'It might.'

'So your father's welfare isn't your main concern after all?'

'Yes! I mean. . . .' She paused, biting her lip. 'You're putting words in my mouth.'

'Whereas you're supposed to be putting food into it. I thought you were hungry?'

Right now the very idea of eating made her throat close up. 'I changed my mind,' she said. 'That's a prerogative I'm still allowed, I take it?'

'Providing it doesn't go too far.' He took the plate from her, signalling to a waiter. 'Buffet food does nothing for my palate either. If your appetite has returned by the time we reach the hotel, we'll have something brought up.'

It was still only a little after ten o'clock when they found their host and hostess to say goodnight. Indecently early, Lauren gathered from the protestations understandable in any language. She was glad to don the protecting cloak again and make her escape, although with Nick at her back there was no freedom.

They were alone in the lift going up to their suite. At this hour all of Rome would be at dinner. Nick had seemed cool and collected during the whole of the journey back to the hotel. It was doubly a shock when he took hold of her the moment the door was closed and pulled her roughly into his arms.

The kiss numbed her with its fierceness, robbing her of any last lingering hope that her captor may suffer a change of heart.

'That was for encouraging Macchioni,' he said unfairly when he let her go. The rest will be for me.' He took the cloak from her, eyes kindling as he looked at her. 'I hope you're not going to start protesting about your empty stomach now we're here, because I'm not disposed to wait.'

'I'm not going to start protesting anything,' Lauren denied through stiff lips. 'What use would it be?'

'What use indeed!' They were still standing in the little lobby. Quite gently, he turned her about, drawing down the long zip which stretched from her nape to the base of her spine, a finger tip following on to trace the latter with a touch so delicate she almost thought she had imagined it. 'Beautiful,' he murmured. 'As supple as a willow!'

Lauren forced herself to stand rigidly still as he slid the clinging gold material down her arms and over her hips, feeling it glide the rest of the way down her legs to the floor. Clad only in the single brief silk garment, she closed her eyes and waited, pulses leaping as his hands came around her waist and lifted to cup her breasts. His lips were at her nape, parting her hair with a brushing motion until they reached the soft skin beneath, his tongue finding the tiny nerve ends and springing them alive. She told herself it was the air-conditioning that made her shiver, but her body felt hot. Her limbs began giving way, allowing her to sag closer against him. She fought the urgent desire to tear his hands away from her, suspecting that any such action would only serve to inflame him further. She had to allow him to do as he willed without any reaction on her part. Only that way could she retain any command of the situation at all.

She was only half prepared when he swung her up into his arms to carry her into the bedroom. He hadn't bothered to switch on any lights and the darkness was

more than welcome. Laying her on the bed, he stood
back to take off his tuxedo, dropping it carelessly to the
floor and following it with the cummmerbund from
about his waist. His shoes were next, then came tie and
shirt. Lauren kept her eyes fixed straight ahead as he
slid the zip on his trousers, feverishly channelling her
thoughts away from the coming moments. It was only
around nine o'clock back home. Dinner over, Carol
and her father would probably be sharing a quiet drink
together, or even playing Scrabble in the firelight. No,
they would be watching the news on television,
wouldn't they? Dad always watched the nine o'clock
broadcast when he was at home. If they were at home,
of course. Perhaps they'd gone out to a concert.
Tuesday nights they often did. Tuesday? Had she really
only arrived in Rome that afternoon? It seemed like a
hundred years!

The warmth and weight of the body coming down on
top of her broke up her thoughts into a thousand
jumbled pieces. Supporting himself on his elbows, Nick
traced kisses from the point of her jaw down her throat
to her breasts, nuzzling between them to find the arch
of bone beneath the flesh before beginning to explore
the curves to either side of his mouth. Lauren stiffened
involuntarily as his lips touched her nipple, feeling it
peak and harden to the caress. Closing her eyes, she
tried to concentrate on something else—anything but
what was happening right here and now. If she was
physically weak that meant emotionally she had to be
twice as strong. He would defile her body but he
couldn't capture her mind.

The caresses began changing character when there
was no response from her, growing rougher and more
demanding. She gasped as his hand tore away the flimsy
briefs, but still made no move to stop him.

The knee thrust suddenly between her legs had a strength of purpose not to be resisted even if she had intended trying. 'If this is the way you want it,' he gritted.

Lauren bit down hard on her lower lip as he forced her to yield to him, stifling the moan of pain. The driving pressure of his body bore her down into the mattress, rending her asunder. She wanted to scream a protest at the sheer violation, but there was no breath left in her.

It was over quickly. Nick didn't linger, rolling away from her to lie totally still except for the heavy rise and fall of his chest. Lauren felt cold and clammy, her body bruised. She had retained her scanty control of the situation, but what had it gained her? Certainly she had little pride left.

'Why did you make yourself out to be what you're obviously not?' he asked harshly after a moment or two, breaking the silence between them. 'You never had a man before, did you?'

Her throat hurt, but she answered with contempt. 'You didn't give me the impression it mattered one way or the other to you when I told you on the plane this morning.'

'I didn't believe you, that's why.'

She said thickly, 'You mean it might have stopped you if you had?'

'Not necessarily,' he admitted. But I'd have used a little more finesse. As it was, by the time I realised it was too late.' He rolled to look at her, his breath coming warm on her cheek. 'You didn't answer the question. Why the act?'

'It wasn't an act, just an assumption on your part.' She attempted to sit up prior to getting off the bed, recoiling abruptly as his hand came out to grasp her shoulder. 'Don't touch me!' she spat at him. 'I can't bear you to touch me!'

'Hardly surprising considering.' He made no attempt to remove the restraining hand. 'You didn't even wait to hear what I had to say before offering yourself. What was I supposed to think?'

'You're looking for excuses,' she said, 'but there aren't any. It comes out rape in any language!'

'You asked for it.' The harshness was back. 'So don't look for apologies.'

'I wouldn't waste my time.' She drew in a shuddering breath. 'There isn't much point in keeping me with you now, is there? I'm obviously not equipped to provide the kind of entertainment you were hoping for.'

It was a moment or two before he answered that one, his expression difficult to define in the darkness. 'You don't really expect me to put you on a plane home,' he stated flatly at length. 'We made a bargain. It still stands.'

Lauren gazed at him helplessly, the faint hope fading. 'You won't make me give in to you,' she said. 'All you'll get from me is more of the same!'

'I doubt it.' The tone had a dry edge. 'You're not frigid, Lauren. Your body was saying yes if your mind was fighting the inclination. I don't know why you've steered clear of sex up to now, and I don't particularly want to know. Having broken the ice, so to speak, I think I'm entitled to take you the rest of the way.'

'I steered clear,' she responded tautly, 'because I never found one man I could put any trust in!'

'Including your father?'

'Leave him out of it!'

'How can I?' he demanded. 'He's the whole reason you're here with me now. Would you rather I'd followed my original intention and turned him over to the proper authorities?'

The tension drained out of her suddenly, leaving her as deflated as a pierced balloon. 'No,' she admitted.

'Well, then, start showing a little gratitude.'

'Has there ever been a woman in your life you didn't despise?' she asked huskily as his lips found bare flesh again, but he ignored the question. This time his handling was gentler, eliciting a certain response in spite of her determination.

'You can't fight both of us,' he murmured. 'Let me show you what it can be like.'

'I don't want to know,' she denied thickly. 'Not from you!'

'You'll change your mind.' There was confidence in the statement. 'I'll make you change your mind!'

He came very close to it in the following moments, Lauren was bound to acknowledge. There was no actual physical pain when he claimed her again, but the need inside her was almost as bad.

'It's a start,' he declared cynically afterwards. 'You can fight it but you can't win. You don't have what it takes.'

Lauren gazed numbly at the ceiling as he turned his back on her to pummel his pillow in readiness for sleep. Feeling the way she did about him, it should have been easy to reject him, but reason seemed to have little to do with it. It was going to be a case not of whether she could hold out against him, but for how long.

# CHAPTER FIVE

THE bed beside her was empty when Lauren awoke, with only the dent in the pillow to show where the arrogant dark head had rested. The note propped against her bedside lamp robbed her of any fleeting hope that Nick had left her for good.

*Back for lunch,* she read. *Stay put.*

It was nine-thirty—later by far than she was accustomed to rising. The exhaustion had been as much mental as physical, she realised. Even now she felt dull and depressed.

Instinctively she sought comfort. The note had said wait, but that didn't necessarily mean what she took it to mean. Last night Nick had been angry because he had felt she had made a fool of him; in the light of day he may be more amenable. If his main reason for wanting her with him had been to put down Francesca, then she had already served her purpose.

She was living in a fool's paradise, and she knew it. Nick had no intention of letting her go. Not until his male ego had been properly restored. Looking into lacklustre green eyes in the dressing-table mirror, she wondered if she would have felt any better had she provided that satisfaction. Certainly she could feel no worse. Nick was an experienced man-of-the-world. Given the right kind of incentive, he could make the experience worth remembering.

And meaningless, another part of her mind reminded her. Had sexual fulfilment been her only aim she could no doubt have known that a dozen times with a dozen

68

different men. What she wanted—what she had always wanted—was love to go with it. Was that such a foolish desire in this day and age?

Arguing with herself this way was getting her nowhere, she decided abruptly. Until Nick returned she couldn't be sure of his plans for the immediate future. She could cling to hope even if deep down she believed it a waste of time.

The pearl-and-gold pendant still hung about her neck. Lauren had to struggle with the clasp but she got it open eventually, depositing the piece on the dressing table along with the bracelet. Beautiful, she supposed, but after this she would never be able to look at pearls without remembering. No doubt Nick would be returning both items to the place he had bought them from. She had no desire to wear them again.

Showered and dressed in cream cotton, she felt refreshed in body if not in spirit. The view from the sitting-room window was colossal. From where she stood she could look down across the Colosseum to the impressive ruins of the Forum, both bathed in bright sunlight. Two thousand years ago that same sun had lit an Empire in the heyday of its rule. It was difficult to believe that so much time had passed.

Hunger stirred her into picking up the telephone. It was too late for breakfast, but room service was round the clock. Her Italian was equal to ordering coffee and rolls, though only just. She smiled wryly when the man taking her order repeated it in excellent English. She should have known that a hotel this size and calibre would have a linguistic staff.

Nick returned earlier than she had anticipated, to find her out on the balcony watching the flow of traffic along the Via Claudia. She had been unaware of his presence, turning to see him standing in the doorway behind her. The sun caught her hair as she moved, creating a red-gold cloud about her well-shaped head. The expression crossing the lean features was both fleeting and confusing.

'I didn't expect you yet,' she said. 'It's barely eleven.'

'I couldn't wait any longer.' His tone was wry. 'I owe you an apology. I treated you abominably last night.'

She couldn't dispute that statement, nor did she try. The very fact that he was even bothering to apologise was balm to her injured spirit.

'You made a mistake,' she said at length. 'We both did. I should have given you the benefit of the doubt.'

'You don't know the half of it.' The wryness was still there. 'I'd already decided to hold fire where your father was concerned before you turned up with that offer of yours. He's been with the firm a long time. If he'd been doing the same kind of thing on a regular basis he'd have been caught before this.'

Lauren's eyes were dark, her body tensed. 'You mean I needn't have put myself in this position at all?'

'No. The fact that you did. . . .' He paused, shoulders lifting in a gesture which could be construed as defensive. 'You took it for granted I was the kind of man who'd take advantage, so I decided to oblige you. Even then, you might have got away with it if I hadn't heard about Francesca.'

'The phone call?'

He nodded. 'I was expecting Francesca herself. What I got was a mutual friend telling me the news in the hope that I'd have time to adjust to it before leaving for Rome. You were just what I needed to throw in her face.'

'But you weren't in love with her. You told me so.'

Her smile was dry. 'My pride was at stake. For two years I'd been keeping her in luxury; she had everything any woman could want.'

Lauren said softly, 'Except her own pride perhaps.'

'She gave up any right to that a long time ago.' His tone had hardened a fraction. 'I wasn't the first, any more than Luigi will be the last.'

'He married her though. Surely that makes a difference?'

'For a time, maybe. Until she gets desperate. Francesca can no more stay true to one man than fly!'

'Including you?'

The irony was not lost on him. He shrugged again. 'Providing she was there when I wanted her I was willing to turn a blind eye. Luigi won't be prepared to do that. His weapon is money. He'll buy off any other man she finds.'

There was a pause before Lauren said slowly, 'Do I take it I can go home now?'

The grey eyes were unreadable. 'Only if you want to. For myself, I'd like the chance to reform your opinion of me a little.'

She searched his features, her heart suddenly and inexplicably lighter. 'Why?' she whispered.

'Because it matters to me.' He moved forward towards her, putting both hands on her shoulders to look into her face. His smile started bells ringing inside her. This was a different Nick—a man whose attraction she could no longer deny. She had to forcibly remind herself that nothing had really changed.

'Why?' she asked again, trying to sound cool and logical about it. 'Why should it matter to you one way or the other?'

'Because you matter. More than any other woman ever did.' His thumb caressed her cheek, the touch so tender she could scarcely believe it. 'I spent a sleepless night regretting the way we began—regretting so many things. Is it too late to start again?'

'I don't know.' She was finding it difficult to think straight. 'Nick. . . .'

'Perhaps this may help,' he said, and bent his head to find her mouth, cherishing it in a way that made her weak at the knees. She clung to him mindlessly, kissing him back with ever-decreasing reserve, her arms creeping about his neck. This was the way it should be—the way she had known deep down that it could be. Last night seemed like a bad dream.

'I want you very much,' he said softly against her hair some moments later, 'but I'm going to deny myself that pleasure. First we spend time simply getting to know each other. Does that sound good to you?'

She was dazed by the sheer speed with which the whole situation had altered. She said hesitantly, 'I don't think I'm capable of handling an affair, if that's what you have in mind.'

'It isn't.' He was still holding her close, his lips nuzzling her ear. 'Lauren, I'm thirty-four years old—almost thirty-five. I've already sown my share of wild oats. I always promised myself that the girl I eventually married would have to be special. Not just beautiful to look at, but with qualities I could respect. However misguided you were in offering to sell yourself to me, you only did it for your father's sake. As a virgin, it must have been a doubly difficult thing to do.'

Things were moving too fast for her; she could scarcely keep up. 'We're strangers,' she whispered. 'You know nothing about me. Not really.'

'I know enough. Time will take care of the rest.' He held her close, making her aware of his arousal. 'You're undermining my control, *cara*. If we stay here like this for very much longer I won't be responsible for what will surely happen!'

It was partly the unexpected and so tenderly spoken

endearment, partly her own sudden surge of desire that made her say it, her voice so low she could barely hear it herself. 'Then let it happen.'

He laughed then, the sound soft. 'I was hoping you'd say that. I have a lot to make up for!'

The bedroom was cool behind closed shutters, the light filtered to a pearly grey. Nick undressed her slowly, kissing each breast as he bared them, easing any last remaining tension from her body with the gentleness of his touch.

Lauren responded instinctively, her own touch shy at first but growing bolder along with her confidence when he revealed his pleasure. Last night's pain and degradation seemed light years away; today she yearned for the union.

'Not yet,' Nick murmured, kissing her eager mouth. 'I want you to remember this as if it were the first time.' He eased himself up on his elbows to study her, eyes flaming as they followed the smoothly curving lines. His lips traced the same path, making her quiver like an aspen leaf in a breeze, her protest stillborn. There was no reticence left in her, just the shrieking need for fulfilment. When they came together at last it was like the end of the world.

It was a long time before either of them moved or spoke. Lauren felt totally replete, her mind blank of thought. She didn't want to think. Not beyond this moment. It was enough for now that she was with Nick.

It couldn't stay that way, of course. Nick stirred first, albeit with reluctance.

'For a novice you certainly know how to exhaust a man,' he said. 'I can't remember the last time I felt so utterly and completely drained!' He rolled his head in order to see her face, expression oddly uncertain. 'How do you feel?'

'Wonderful!' She stretched luxuriously, conscious of her nudity yet no longer inhibited by it. 'I never realised what I'd been missing.'

'It compensated for last night?'

She looked at him then, sensing a need for reassurance. Her smile supplied it. 'You already compensated for last night. I can imagine what it took for a man like you to apologise—especially to a woman.'

His brows lifted a fraction. 'You really think I'm that chauvinistic?'

She laughed. 'I'm sure of it. Your whole attitude bears that out.' There was a pause. When she spoke again it was on a different note, 'Nick, what you said out there on the balcony. . . .'

'Was meant.' The arm still under her shoulders curved to draw her over towards him, holding her so that they were face to face. His eyes were impenetrable. 'I want you to marry me, Lauren. And soon. Does the idea appeal to you?'

She shook her head in confusion, emotion fighting with reason. 'It's happened too quickly to take in. If it's time for you to take a wife there must be plenty of eminently suitable candidates to choose from.'

He was silent for a moment watching her; he seemed to be considering his approach. 'Last night, you told me I knew nothing of the power of love,' he said at length. 'Last night you were right.'

Lauren stared at him, heart jerking painfully. 'And now?'

The smile warmed her. 'Now, I'm a changed man. The influence of a good woman isn't to be underrated.'

'You're taunting me,' she said, still unable to take what he was saying seriously. Her tone thickened. 'Don't make a joke of it, Nick!'

'I don't intend to.' He took her face between his two hands, the ball of each thumb just touching the corners of her mouth as he kissed it. 'We can be married this afternoon. I already have the licence. All it takes is your agreement.'

'Today!' The sense of unreality was heightened by the minute. 'But. . . .'

'But what?' He kissed her again, scrambling her thoughts. 'We have everything going for us. Why wait?'

There had to be a hundred reasons, yet at that particular moment Lauren couldn't find a single valid one. Did love really happen like this? she wondered dazedly as he fanned her senses alight once more. She knew so little about this man, apart from the fact that he made her feel the way no other had ever made her feel before. He said he loved her. Why should he lie?

Afterwards, Lauren was to wonder if Nick knew anything about hypnotism because she had gone along so blindly with what he asked. They were facing the Italian equivalent of a registrar before she began to question her actions with any real seriousness, and by then it was too late.

Emerging into the hot afternoon sunshine with the man who was now her husband, she thought for the first time in hours of her father, trying to imagine his reaction to the news. How did she explain something she barely understood herself?

And what about the job in Brussels? Had she gone mad doing a thing like this! There was neither rhyme nor reason to it.

Nick hailed a cruising taxi-cab, putting her into it and giving the driver the name of their hotel before joining her in the back.

'You're shaking,' he said quietly. 'It's too late for second thoughts, Lauren.'

'I know.' It was all she could do to force the words out. 'I'm sorry. It all happened so fast. I can't take it in yet.'

'You're my wife.' The tone was firm. 'Is the thought so bad?'

She made no immediate answer, looking out through the window with blank, unseeing eyes. 'How did you manage it?' she asked at length. 'I'd have thought here in Italy it took time to arrange a marriage.'

'A little greasing of palms eases the passage of paperwork miraculously,' came the cynical reply. 'It's still legal. I assure you.'

The faint hope died before it was properly born. Lauren wasn't even certain what it was she had wanted to hear. 'I had a job to go to,' she said. 'To say nothing of what I tell my father.'

Nick smiled briefly. 'Tell him you were swept off your feet. I'll take care of the Brussel end. There's no great shortage of good stenographers.'

'Bi-lingual ones?' she asked with an edge. 'Don't sell me short, Nick!'

'I wouldn't even try.' He reached out and took her hand, enfolding it in his palm. 'There's no going back, *cara*—for either of us.'

Her head came round then as if jerked by an invisible wire, her eyes searching his face in sudden swift panic. 'You're having regrets?'

He returned her gaze levelly. 'That isn't what I said.'

'It's what you implied.'

'Not that either.' The smile came again. 'I was the one who instigated the whole thing, remember? Do I strike you as lacking in stability?'

'No,' she acknowledged.

'Well then?'

'It's different, isn't it?'

'How is it different?'

Lauren searched her mind desperately for some way of expressing what she wanted to say. 'Anyone is capable of being carried away by impulse,' was the only thing she could come up with.

'Except that I obtained the licence and made the arrangements before I even saw you again, much less made love to you. Does that sound like impulse?'

Green eyes looked into grey, seeking some insight to the man within. 'You were so certain I was going to say yes?'

'I was so certain I wasn't going to let you say no,' he returned equably. 'Relax, will you. Everything is going to be all right. Tomorrow we go to Venice.'

'Venice?'

'The family home.'

Lauren sighed, sinking back into her seat. 'There's so much I don't know about you. I had the impression you were estranged from your Italian relatives. You said last night you only had yourself to consider.'

'I wasn't talking about the same thing.' His tone was dry. 'Grandfather will expect to meet my bride.'

'If he ever finds out how we met he'll hardly approve,' she murmured.

'So who's going to tell him? So far as anyone else is concerned, we simply met and fell in love. The romance alone will provide enough intrigue.'

She glanced at him sharply, to meet the same enigmatic gaze. 'Do you have to sound so cynical about it?'

'Is that how it sounded?' He laughed and shook his head. 'It wasn't intended.'

Lauren wasn't so sure. But then what was she sure

of? Since waking this morning her whole life had been turned upside down.

'Stop worrying, will you?' Nick's voice was gentle enough to remind her of what he could be like when moved the right way. 'You're Lauren Brent, a respectable married woman.'

'They won't know that at the hotel though, will they?' she said.

'Not unless I announce it.' He was half amused, half impatient. 'What does it matter? We'll only be there one more night.' His tone softened again at the look on her face. 'This evening we'll celebrate. Just the two of us. I know just the place.'

'You won't expect me to wear the same dress, I hope,' she said, and saw the wry smile form once more.

'Never again,' he promised. 'In Venice you can do your own shopping—buy whatever takes your fancy.'

Something in his tone prompted the question. 'How long are you planning on staying? After all, you still have to complete your tour of the European branches.'

'There's no rush. The itinerary was very flexible.'

There was something evasive about the reply. She said slowly, 'If it was your grandfather who helped persuade your mother to bring you back to Italy I'd have thought you'd still hold him responsible.'

Nick shrugged, expression difficult to define. 'There comes a time when the past has to be put aside.'

Lauren could only agree with that philosophy, so why should the vague sense of unease still linger? She was picking up nuances where none existed, she decided. If she wanted to worry about something, there was the problem of when and how she informed her father of the change in circumstances. No matter how she did it, it was going to be a shock. Perhaps if she phoned Carol first. At least the latter was aware of her whereabouts.

The taxi was coming to a stop outside the hotel. She waited on the pavement for Nick to pay the driver. It was still only twenty minutes past four. Carol and her father would be back from lunch and at their respective desks by now. For a fleeting moment she wished she could turn back the clock to that time less than a week ago when she had first set eyes on Nick. Not that it would have made a great deal of difference without pre-knowledge of what was to come.

Regardless of its size, the suite itself seemed claustrophobic once the outer door was closed. Cutting off her line of escape, Lauren told herself with a rueful inward smile. She turned gratefully to Nick when he took her in his arms, lifting her face eagerly to his kiss. Close to him like this she could think of little else.

'I'm going to take a shower,' he said softly when he let her go. 'Come with me.'

Lauren shook her head, not yet quite ready for that degree of intimacy. 'I have to tell them at home sometime. It may as well be right away.'

His smile was not without irony. 'Next time then. Making love under running water is something special. Tell your father he doesn't have anything to worry about. All I'll want from him is his cheque for the basic amount when the time comes.'

'What about the profit?' Lauren asked tentatively. 'He won't want to keep it. Not now. The whole thing was a temporary derangement. He regretted the investment the same day he made it, only it was too late to withdraw.'

'If the Company follows my recommendations, no one man will ever have the power to utilise funds from any source again.' Nick's tone was level. 'What he does with the profit is his own concern. Let his conscience decide.'

Lauren sat for several moments in the sitting room plucking up the courage to lift the telephone receiver and ask the operator to make the connection. The call would be picked up by Carol anyway; there was no danger of hearing her father's voice directly on the line. Whether she could bring herself to speak to him at all was the main problem, although leaving Carol to explain the situation was hardly fair to either of them.

In the end she forced herself to make the move, waiting interminable minutes for the clicking, buzzing line to produce results. At length there came the familiar ringing tone, then a click as the receiver was lifted at the other end of the line and the calm, efficient tones: 'Grantley, Brent, Taylor; Mr Devlin's office.'

'Go ahead caller,' intoned the British operator, and Lauren drew in a steadying breath.

'Carol, it's me.'

'Lauren?' The coolness was gone, taken over by concern, warm and reassuring. 'Where are you?'

'In a hotel.'

'Alone?'

'At the moment.' It was difficult to know how to broach the subject. She tried leading up to it by stages. 'Is Dad in?'

'Not right now. He took a client to lunch. They haven't got back yet.' There was an expectant pause. 'Lauren? You still there?'

'I'm still here,' Lauren said. Her father's absence made things easier in one sense and harder in another. She had two choices now: she could either tell Carol the whole story and leave it to her to pass on, or she could ring back later. She made a swift decision, trying to justify it by telling herself she had to tell Carol something. 'A lot's happened,' she began. 'I ... It's going to be a bit of a shock. I'm still recovering from it myself.'

'What is it?' Carol sounded concerned. 'Has that man harmed you?'

The laugh was forced. 'On the contrary, he married me. Just an hour ago. Can you believe it?'

The silence seemed to go on for ever. Lauren had just begun to think they had been disconnected when Carol said slowly, 'You're not joking, are you? You really mean it!'

'I really mean it.' She swallowed on dryness. 'I know how it must sound, but it happened so fast between us. One minute I was hating him, the next. . . .'

'The next you were both so madly in love you had to make it legal?' The scepticism came through loud and clear. 'Lauren, that only happens in fairy tales!'

'It's the truth. And it was all Nick's idea.'

'All inside of twenty-four hours?'

'Less than that actually. It was only after. . . .' Lauren broke off, realising there were some things that could not be discussed over an open line. She tried again. 'It's impossible to make anyone else understand. I'm only just beginning to take it in properly myself. When you. . . .'

'Do you love him?' The question was abrupt, breaking her off in mid-sentence.

The hesitation was brief enough to be almost nonexistent. 'Of course I love him! Why else would I have married him?'

'That's what I'm asking myself, and I can't come up with any other answer either.' Another pause before Carol added softly, 'Does he love you?'

'The same answer applies, I suppose.' Lauren hurried on. 'He's taking me to meet his grandfather in Venice tomorrow. He's half Italian, you know.'

'Yes, as a matter of fact I did know. What about your father?'

'That's my greatest problem at the moment. You at least knew I was with Nick. He thinks I'm in Brussels.'

'It might be best if I explained everything to him myself,' said Carol after a moment. 'Perhaps you could contact him from Venice in a couple of days. That will give him time to adjust to the idea.'

Lauren hesitated again, torn between relief and doubt. 'Are you sure?'

'I'm sure. I'll wait till tonight when he has a strong drink to hand. He's going to need it.' The laugh sounded strained. 'I could do with one myself right now!'

'It's going to be all right,' Lauren stated, wishing she could feel quite as certain as she sounded. 'It may have been unorthodox, but I know what I'm doing.'

'I hope so.' Carol sounded doubtful. 'Good luck anyway.'

A wave of homesickness swept over Lauren as she replaced the receiver in its rest. Oh, God, she thought, what am I doing here?

The answer to that question came through from the bedroom, a towelling robe tied loosely about his middle. His hair was damp and curling at the ends. 'Get through okay?' he asked on a casual note.

Looking at him, she felt the hard little knot inside her begin to unfurl, the need to start taking shape. When Nick made love to her nothing else mattered. She wanted him now, and desperately.

'Only to Carol,' she said. 'She's going to tell Dad for me.'

'Fine.' He glanced across at the cabinet where the drinks were stored. 'Feel like a toast?'

'No thanks.' Her voice was low and slightly shaky. 'Nick, will you do something for me?'

He turned to look at her, one eyebrow lifting quizzically. 'What did you have in mind?'

'Just come and hold me.'

His laugh was gently derisive. 'Just that?'

Her colour rose a little, 'No,' she admitted.

'Then say what you really want.' The grey eyes had a taunting gleam. 'Be bold, *cara*. Words can excite the senses as much as action.'

She hadn't meant to say it; the words came of their own accord, 'Did you call Francesca that too?'

His lips thinned suddenly. 'It didn't take long to have you throwing her name in my face! Just forget about Francesca!'

'I'm sorry.' She really meant it. She held out her arms to him, needing reassurance. 'Make love to me, Nick.'

He came to her then, but there was a certain restraint in his kiss as if her remark still rankled. Not that it lasted long. Lauren made sure of that. She was learning fast, her confidence growing. Whatever else she may be unsure of, his physical responses left no room for doubt in her mind.

# CHAPTER SIX

THERE was a party of English tourists on board the ferry from the airport. Listening to their voices, Lauren stifled the pang of homesickness and concentrated on the Canaletto skyline ahead. Torn as she was, she could not fail to appreciate the sheer beauty of the waterfront. They were passing the elegant sculpture of the Doge's Palace; she could see the warm red brick of the bell tower lofting beyond. The Piazetta was awash with human bodies, but nothing could detract from that first glimpse of the famous square framed between the two slender columns. Gondolas rode the incandescent waves, heading to and from the entrance to the Grand Canal away to the left. To imagine living here in such surroundings for even a short time was beyond her. She felt totally lost.

'Stop looking so downcast,' Nick admonished on a note of faint intolerance. 'Nobody's going to eat you!'

'I can't help it,' she said. 'You're springing as great a surprise on your grandfather as I will have done on my father.'

He smiled dryly. 'Not any more. I phoned through this morning while you were in the shower. We're expected.'

Lauren glanced at him swiftly. 'What was the reaction?'

'I didn't speak to Grandfather personally,' he admitted. 'It was too early. He'll have been told by now though, you can be sure.'

It was small comfort at least. She said chidingly, 'You might have told me before this.'

'I might have done a whole lot of things if I'd thought of them in time,' came the somewhat enigmatic response. He was looking shorewards again now, searching the sea of faces thronging the quayside. One hand lifted suddenly in greeting. 'There's Vincenzo!'

'Vincenzo?'

'A distant cousin. His father is the family comptroller. They live at the Palazzo.'

The palace! Lauren's head was reeling. 'You never told me your family belonged to the aristocracy!'

'We never got round to discussing it.' Nick was mildly amused by her stunned expression. 'Don't let imagination run away with you. The family lost any right to the title along with the rest back in the seventeenth century, although some still use them as a status symbol.'

'But your grandfather isn't one of them?'

'No, thank God. As next in line of succession I'd be known as the Marchese di Severino. Hardly my style, is it?' He took hold of her arm. 'They're disembarking. Let's go.'

Vincenzo came forward to greet them after they passed through the terminal. He was younger than Nick by five or six years, and shorter by several inches, but his features were cast in the same chiselled mould. He wore a beautifully tailored pale cream suit with a navy blue shirt and paler tie, contrasting sharply with Nick's casual slacks and shirt. The eyes resting on Lauren's face held an expression she found difficult to assess. Reluctant admiration was the closest she could come.

She gave him her hand in response to Nick's introductions, to have it held fractionally longer than was strictly necessary.

'Nick is a lucky man,' he said in excellent English. 'You are very beautiful.'

Lauren thanked him for the compliment, conscious once more of the inner struggle going on behind those dark eyes. Her presence here was not wholly welcome, that much she could ascertain. She slipped a hand through Nick's arm, feeling the muscle contract beneath his fingers as if in sympathy with her feelings.

'Guido is berthed along the quay,' Vincenzo added, hoisting their two suitcases as the three of them moved away from the crowd passing through to the ferry. He waited a moment before saying expressionlessly, 'The news did not please your grandfather.'

'He'll get over it.' Nick sounded unperturbed. 'He'll have to get over it. The right of succession is one thing he can't take away from me, no matter how far I go against his wishes. Not after three hundred years.'

'You should have come sooner,' murmured Vincenzo. 'It was your duty to be with the family these past years.'

'You know why I preferred to bide my time.' Nick still sounded calm enough but there was a faint edge to his voice. 'Fiorella is free now to look for a husband elsewhere. I'd have thought you'd be thankful.'

The younger man gave him a wry sideways glance. 'The Bianchi family is proud.'

Nick shrugged. 'Aren't they all!'

Lauren had stayed silent all through the little exchange, her mind drawing its own conclusions. Nick had been expected to marry this Fiorella Bianchi, that was apparent. Instead he had preferred to stay away from his Italian family home until he found a woman *he* wanted to marry. She should have found that knowledge reassuring, yet somehow it carried a sting in its tail. She was a statement of independence, that was all.

With some deliberation she slowed her steps, waiting until Vincenzo was ahead of them before saying softly, 'You should have told me what I was getting into. If you were supposed to marry someone else. . . .'

'I never had any intention,' he denied. 'But my grandfather takes a lot of convincing.' He laughed. 'You're my ace in the hole!'

'To be shuffled back into the pack as soon as I've served my purpose?' The words were out before she had time to give them any real thought.

The laughter died, the grey eyes turning to steel. 'If that's your considered opinion there isn't much point in my denying it.'

'Nick, I'm sorry.' Impulsively she caught his arm again. 'I feel so insecure, that's all.'

'You don't have any reason to feel insecure. You're my legal wife.' The coolness was still there behind the smile. 'Just remember that.'

They followed Vincenzo out along a wooden landing-stage to where one of the long, black-painted gondolas was tied. Unlike many of the others, it had a tasselled and fringed canopy over the wrought-iron seating. The man standing on the stern cover holding the craft steady against the current with his long wooden oar was dressed in black and gold livery, his whole demeanour one of aloofness from the other gondolieri in the vicinity. Stepping down into the gently rocking boat with Vincenzo's assistance, Lauren noted the crest at the head of the thickly padded, wrought-iron seats, the richness of the hangings. The Marchese di Severino—what would that have made her? She was thankful the title no longer existed. Even plain Mrs Brent sounded alien enough right now.

It was surprisingly choppy on the open water when they first pulled out from the protection of the berth.

Lauren clutched the ornate arm of her chair and tried not to think about capsising. Behind and above, she could hear the exhale of breath each time Guido drove the long single sweep back in its pivot to propel them forward, and recalled the muscular development of his shoulders and upper arms, visible even beneath the material of his livery.

'There is no danger,' Vincenzo assured her with a reassuring smile as they took another wave against the side. 'You have never visited Venice before?'

'Never,' Lauren acknowledged, returning the smile. 'Although I always wanted to come sometime.'

'And now it will be your home.' The wry quality was back for a moment in his voice. 'I hope you will be happy here.'

Home? Lauren sent a swift glance in Nick's direction, to have it returned without expression. He had said nothing about living here permanently. Vincenzo must be mistaken. They would be returning to England, of course. They had to go back! Nick's job was there.

The Grand Canal lived up to its name. To either side of the wide expanse, buildings crowded to the water's edge, the peeling paint and stucco failing to detract from the overall beauty of the architecture. A vaporetto slid past, packed from end to end with travellers heading for the pool of St Mark. The sound of a guitar played with both skill and verve floated across the water.

Lauren sat entranced as they journeyed, struck dumb by the sheer quality of light and colour under the clear blue sky. This was the Venice of all her anticipations, shabby in parts yet timeless in its appeal to the senses. For the moment she could even forget the reason she was here and simply enjoy the sensation.

They left the main canal shortly after passing beneath the Accademia Bridge, turning left into a narrower yet no less arresting waterway to glide almost immediately through an arch beneath a tall, Gothic building and into a high-ceilinged cellar. A stone landing-stage was backed by a flight of steps leading up to double doors in the far wall. Even as the boat came to a halt, the former opened, and a manservant wearing the black-and-gold livery of the household came down the steps to take the suitcases handed to him by Guido.

Nick was the first out of the gondola, leaning down to help Lauren on to dry land. A sleek motor launch was moored to an iron ring in the stone wall some little distance away. Guido went to tie up alongside it.

The stone steps were damp, their treads deeply worn in the middle by the pressure of countless feet. The manservant had left the doors ajar. Passing through them, Lauren found herself in a room of such outstanding beauty she could only stare in amazement. The ceiling was high and vaulted, its surface covered in superb paintings, each enclosed within a gilded framework in high relief. On all four walls were frescoes so bright and clear they could have been painted only yesterday, extending right down to the gilded panelling. The floor underfoot was finest ivory marble, ringing to the sound of Lauren's heels as she moved forward in dazed wonder.

'It's superb!' she breathed. 'Nick, how absolutely lovely!'

'Yes, it is, isn't it.' He seemed almost amused by her reaction. 'I never could learn to take it for granted the way Vincenzo here does.'

'Not true,' declared the other man without heat. 'It is simply that I see it every day of my life. Carlo will have taken your baggage straight to your room. You would like to go there first and freshen up after your journey?'

'It might be a good idea,' agreed Nick casually. 'Where did you put us?'

'The Blue Chamber.' Where else? Vincenzo's tone suggested. 'Your grandfather will be taking siesta until four o'clock,' he added. 'He tires easily these days.'

'We shan't disturb him.' Nick's tone was suddenly shorter. 'I know where the room is, so don't let us keep you any longer. No doubt we'll see you later.'

'At dinner,' the other agreed. He seemed about to say something else, then apparently changed his mind, moving off across the hall instead.

Lauren waited until they were halfway up the imposing staircase before saying tentatively, 'Vincenzo seems to think you're going to be staying here for good, Nick. He's wrong, isn't he?'

'Not necessarily.' The statement was perfectly calm. 'It depends on whether Grandfather is willing to accept a *fait accompli* or not. Not that he really has a great deal of choice when it comes right down to it.' His smile was dry. 'You'd better be prepared for a pretty severe interview. He's going to be asking some pertinent questions.'

'To which I'm supposed to answer what?' she demanded, stopping on the curve of the stairs to face him in a mixture of anger and dismay. 'Why didn't you tell me about all this before we came?'

The grey eyes were steady. 'Because I might have lost you,' he said. 'I needed you, Lauren. Too much to take the risk. Is the thought of living here in Venice with me so abhorrent?'

'Your job?' she stammered, side-stepping the question. 'You have a life back home in England. What about all that?'

'Expendable.' He was watching her closely, as if

trying to read some message in her eyes. 'You didn't answer me.'

'I don't know.' She made a helpless little gesture. 'Not abhorrent, no, of course not, but. . . .'

'But not appealing either.' His attitude had hardened again. He gave a faint shrug. 'You married me of your own free will. I used no coercion.'

The words were forced from stiff lips. 'That wasn't what I meant.' She searched his features, trying to find the man in whose arms she had known such certainty of mind; seeing only a stranger. 'Nick, I. . . .'

'Give it time,' he advised, sounding suddenly weary. 'One day we may both find what we're looking for.'

He turned then and continued on up the stairs. Lauren followed him slowly, her emotions in a turmoil. Right now she wasn't even sure what it was she *was* looking for. All she could be certain of was that she had landed herself in a situation from which there was no easy way out.

The Blue Chamber was smaller than she had anticipated—almost cosy, in fact—its panelled walls lined with embroidered silk, its furnishing rich in lacquer. The bed was a four-poster, draped to match the window hangings in blue brocade, the carpet so thick it deadened all sound. A large adjoining closet had been converted into a bathroom, with incongruous modern fittings. To step into it was like travelling through time.

Lauren busied herself unpacking her suitcase while Nick washed and changed, reluctant to share. Only when he returned to the bedroom did she pick up her things, avoiding his eyes as she passed him. Last night, even this morning, she had felt so differently about him. Perhaps tonight when he took her in his arms again that feeling would return, but for the moment she wanted no contact.

He was dressed in a light suit she hadn't seen before when she at length went back to the bedroom. She herself was wearing the pale cream skirt and matching shirt which had been the only items in her case she had felt were even remotely suitable to the occasion.

'I hope this will do,' she said, smoothing the material over her hips. 'I'm afraid I don't have very much else.'

'You look fine,' Nick assured her. He too seemed to be keeping his distance, expression remote. 'Tomorrow I'll get Donata to take you on a shopping trip. Vincenzo's sister,' he added before she could ask the obvious question. 'The family have their own apartment.'

'How is it that you're next in line to succeed your grandfather?' she asked curiously. 'Didn't he have any sons?'

'Only one, and he died in a motor accident. My mother was the second born, and the last. My grandmother would have risked her life having more children, but Grandfather wouldn't allow it.' He was looking in a mirror, hairbrush in hand. Without turning, he added cynically, 'Maybe he'd have changed his mind if he'd realised what the future held. As it is, there's no way he can alter things. That's why he had to bring my mother back into the family when Uncle Giuseppe died without having produced a son. In the Severino lineage only the males inherit.'

'And if you decided against it?'

'Vincenzo would be next in line, through his mother. There was an unfortunate period for the family when sons were at a premium, it seems.' He turned to look at her, brows lifted sardonically at the expression on her face. 'Starting to feel sorry for Vincenzo?'

'No,' she said steadily. 'Why should I? I was just

thinking what a pity that the name has to die out after all this time.'

'It doesn't,' he said. 'On the day I inherit I also adopt the Severino title.'

'In place of Brent?'

'In addition to it, although I'd be addressed as Signor di Severino in this country, naturally.' The smile was lacking in humour. 'What you could call having the best of both worlds.'

'You mean you'll be sharing your time between them?'

'Only in so far as visiting would be concerned.' He shook his head at her. 'You're getting the wrong impression. Grandfather is only seventy. So far as I know, he has no intention of dying for a long time to come.'

'Then why do you need to stay here at all just yet?'

'Because it's time I began learning to take up the mantle.' His tone was firm. 'My only reason for staying away was Fiorella. She no more wanted to marry me than I did her, but they'd have worn us down given half a chance.'

Lauren didn't move. 'But now you're safe because you already have a wife.'

'That's right.' He watched her for a moment, some expression she couldn't define flickering across his face. When he did speak it was softly. 'Come here.'

A part of her wanted badly to obey that summons, but some stronger emotion held her back. 'For what?'

'Because I asked you,' he said. 'Isn't that reason enough?'

It would have been more than enough if their marriage had been a normal one, she thought ruefully. As it was, there was nowhere else to go.

He put a hand under her chin when she reached him,

tilting her face so that he could see it clearly. 'You feel you've been tricked into coming here with me, is that it?' he asked.

'A little.' Lauren looked back at him unsteadily, wishing she could penetrate the veiled gaze. 'When you asked me to marry you, was it only because of this situation?'

He laughed then, sliding the back of his fingers down the line of her throat in a gesture which made her quiver, then taking her by the shoulders to turn her about so that she faced the mirror he had recently used. 'Look at yourself,' he said, 'and tell me the answer to that question.'

She swallowed, suddenly hating the familiar oval face and clouded red-gold hair. 'Looks aren't everything.'

'They're important to me,' he said. 'I couldn't have married a woman I didn't find attractive, no matter how great the incentive.'

'But you don't love me.' It was flat statement.

Something flickered deep down. 'No more or less than you love me,' he countered smoothly. 'Given the opportunity, love can grow between two people.'

It was what she had known in her heart so she had no cause to feel cheated, Lauren told herself. Nick was right, she wasn't in love with him. Not the way she should be. She had married him because she hadn't been able to say no to him—not in any sense of the word. Now she had to learn to live with that knowledge.

'Don't look so sad,' he chided. 'We still have this. . . .' His fingers brushed aside the material of her blouse, baring the delicate line of her collar bone to his lips. Lauren closed her eyes and let the sensation wash through her, willing herself to forget what was lacking from their relationship. She had never wanted to go to Brussels anyway.

They were summoned to the presence promptly at four. Ushered ahead of Nick through the door of the third-floor apartment, Lauren found herself in a room lined with books of all shapes and sizes. The musty smell of ancient leather and parchment permeated the air.

At any other time her gaze would have lingered on the magnificent crystal chandelier hanging from the painted ceiling, on the beautifully carved and inlaid wood of the furnishings. For the present her whole attention was focused on the man standing with his back turned towards them at one of the tall, arched windows. He was little more than medium height, and slight in build, yet the fine head of almost pure white hair gave him presence. She was prepared for the animosity in his eyes when he turned to look at the pair of them.

'Grandfather, I'd like you to meet my wife, Lauren,' said Nick with slow deliberation. 'She speaks no Italian, so I'd be grateful if you would speak English.'

'If we can learn other languages,' said the old man coldly, 'why cannot the English?'

'I speak French fluently, *signor*,' Lauren responded swiftly before Nick could answer for her. 'Italian shouldn't present too much of a problem.'

'Should you stay long enough to learn,' came the discouraging reply. 'It is not merely the language to which you are alien, it is a whole way of life.'

'She'll stay,' Nick stated. 'We both will—providing you allow it. I don't have the power to insist.'

'I am grateful that you recognise your position,' said his grandfather dryly. 'I could turn you away, yes, but it would be little comfort on my deathbed to know that my successor was totally in ignorance of his duties.

There is much to learn, both here in Venice and on our estates in the Veneto.'

There was a pause before Nick replied. He was watching the older man with narrowed eyes. 'You're giving up that easily?' he asked. 'I can hardly believe it.'

The answering smile had a sadness that made Lauren's heart ache. 'I have no choice in the matter. No more than you intended I should have. The only thing I ask . . .' his tone hardened suddenly again, 'no, *insist*, is that the marriage should be consecrated in church, and at the earliest opportunity.' He didn't wait for any reply, his eyes coming back to Lauren without warmth. 'You are very lovely, but then I would have expected that much. Are you comfortable in your room?'

'Very, thank you.' Lauren scarcely knew what else to say. She attempted a smile of her own. 'It's a beautiful place.'

'But of course. The di Severinos have always possessed an aesthetic eye. Nicholas is no exception, even though his blood is diluted.' The pause was brief, the atmosphere no less chilly. 'We know little about you, Perhaps. . . .'

'Anything you need to know, I can tell you,' put in Nick brusquely.

'I don't mind answering questions,' said Lauren as calmly as she was able. 'I don't have anything to hide.' She kept her eyes fixed on the fine patrician face. 'My father is Chief Accountant with Grantley, Brent, Taylor in London; my mother died ten years ago. I'm twenty-three years old, and I'm trained in secretarial work. I speak French as well as English, but unfortunately not Italian too, although I'm more than willing to learn. Apart from that there isn't a great deal to tell. My family name never had any historical significance—at least not that I'm aware of.'

There was a short silence after she had finished speaking. The other's expression was odd. 'You would deny that you married my grandson for wealth and title?' he demanded.

'Yes, I would.' Lauren kept her tone level, her gaze steady. 'I knew he was half Italian but nothing else. In any case, I understand the title no longer has any meaning, so why should I covet it?'

'Why indeed?' Just for a moment there was a glimmer of something approaching humour in his glance. 'You were aware that Nicholas was already betrothed to another?'

'But not with my consent,' put in the latter without undue haste. 'The days of arranged marriages are long gone.'

'Not for all.' Sudden weariness infiltrated the other voice. 'There is little to be gained from debating the point.' He waved a dismissive hand. 'You will please excuse me now. I have letters to write.'

They were outside the door before Lauren drew breath. Stealing a sideways glance at Nick, she saw that he too looked bemused.

'You were expecting him to put up more of a fight, weren't you?' she said. 'He's knocked you for six.'

The smile was wry. 'I'll say one thing for the old devil, he knows when he's beaten!'

'He wasn't beaten,' she said softly. 'Just making the best of things. Nick, he isn't in the least what I expected.'

Grey eyes went flinty. 'You don't know him.'

'Are you sure you do?'

He turned on her then, mouth taut as a bowstring. 'Whose side are you on?'

'No one's. She refused to let her own gaze flicker away. 'I didn't ask to be involved.'

'You married me. That surely allows me some claim on your loyalty?'

'Only where I feel you're in the right.'

'And you don't?'

'Not entirely.' She was struggling for the nerve to see this through. 'If you're so keen on taking over control of the family Empire someday, you should have been prepared to make some sacrifice yourself. Your marriage to Fiorella Bianchi would have satisfied everybody.'

'Except me.' The mockery was in his eyes and his voice. 'She rouses nothing in me, whereas you. . . .' He took hold of her, pressing her back against the gilded panelling to find her mouth in a kiss that hurt. 'You won't leave me,' he said roughly when he lifted his head again. 'I won't let you go!'

'I don't want to leave you.' She was only telling a half truth, because right then her body was saying one thing and her mind another. She looked up into his face, wondering if there would ever come a time when she would really know this man she had married. 'Nick. . . .'

'Don't say it.' His tone had softened as his body had hardened. 'Just come upstairs.'

# CHAPTER SEVEN

IT was dark when Lauren awoke. For a moment she was disorientated, not really certain that any of the impressions in her mind were real and not the figments of dreams. It took the slight movement of the man at her side on the bed to convince her that she was not at home in her own bedroom. She froze, reluctant to have him waken before she had gathered herself together.

In Nick's arms she had been aware of nothing but the emotion of the moment. Their lovemaking had been almost frenzied. Even now she could feel herself go hot and cold at the memory. That she stirred him there was no doubt, but was it really any different for him than it would have been with any other woman he found sexually desirable? He was a man who had known many women—and no doubt become bored with many women too. What happened if and when he lost interest in her that way? They had nothing else to fall back on.

'What time is it?' he asked suddenly, making her wonder how long he had been awake. 'There's a clock on your side.'

Lauren twisted her body to look, reading the figures on the nonilluminated dial with difficulty. 'It's a quarter to eight!' she exclaimed on a note of disbelief.

Nick caught her shoulder as she began to sit up, pulling her back down and turning her across his bare chest so that her mouth was within reach. The kiss was long and lazy.

'What's the hurry?' he asked on a taunting note. 'Dinner isn't until nine. They eat late here.'

'It's still *they*, isn't it?' she said. 'How long before you'll be able to bring yourself to say "*we*"?'

He was silent for a moment, still holding her. When he spoke again his tone was appreciably cooler. 'Maybe never. What difference does it make?'

'A whole lot, I'd have thought, if you're seriously planning on spending the rest of your life here.' Lauren hesitated, the idea only just taking shape. 'Are you really planning on that, Nick—or is this just your way of getting back at your grandfather?'

He moved abruptly, sliding from under her to get to his feet. 'Forget the psychoanalysis, will you. The family usually meet for drinks in the salon around eight-thirty. It's the one time of the day when everyone is together.'

'What do I wear?' Lauren asked resignedly as he walked naked across the room.

He answered without turning his head. 'The blue thing you wore last night will do. It isn't a dressy affair unless visitors are expected.'

He disappeared into the bathroom, leaving Lauren to push herself reluctantly to her own feet. Vincenzo would surely have mentioned it had any occasion been planned, although it would make little difference anyway as the blue dress was all she had. The sparseness of her wardrobe, so deliberately designed, seemed ridiculous in retrospect. Her own pride had suffered far more than Nick's from her lack of attractive outfits. She had the wherewithal to purchase more, but she doubted if Nick was going to allow it. Telling herself she was his wife and entitled to his provision was one thing, accepting it quite another. She didn't feel married.

Recalling what Signor di Severino had said about a second wedding in church, she wondered numbly if that would really make things any better. He had been perfectly serious there was no doubt, yet would Nick be prepared to accept the edict? No matter what happened, he couldn't be disinherited, that was fast becoming clear. Only if he himself renounced all title could the line of descent be altered. He had given her no straight answer to that question, she realised, which left the whole subject open to conjecture. He didn't belong here that was certain. His English half ruled far too strongly.

The large salon ran the full width of the first floor, its heavily draped windows facing out on to the Grand Canal. At first glance the room seemed full of people. Only as her nerve steadied did Lauren realise there were no more than five, two of whom she had already met.

Signor and Signora Laurentiis were a sedate and prosperous-looking couple in their early fifties, their daughter a pretty girl of around Lauren's own age. The latter's greeting was devoid of any rancour, her smile embracing both Lauren and Nick with the same unaffected warmth. Like the rest of her family, she spoke good if somewhat stilted English.

'I look forward to improving my command of your language now that you and Nicholas are here,' she said. 'We shall be good friends, yes?'

'I'm sure we shall,' Lauren replied, grateful for the welcome. 'Perhaps you could help me to learn Italian too.'

'Of course!' Donata's lovely eyes sparkled. 'It will not be difficult when you hear it spoken around you every day. Zio Vittore has told us you are already fluent in French.'

'I'd like you to take Lauren out shopping tomorrow,' Nick cut in smoothly. 'Show her the Venetian fashions. She never got round to buying a trousseau.'

'Perhaps because you gave her no time,' said his grandfather on a caustic note.

'I supose that's right.' Nick's tone was bland. 'I swept her off her feet in true di Severino style!' He slid an arm about Lauren's shoulders, his smile white. 'Isn't that so?'

Lauren wondered fleetingly what the reaction would be if she told them the truth, but her courage wasn't equal to the challenge. When all was said and done, she came out of it all in little better light than Nick himself.

'I'm still reeling,' she said with just enough irony to elicit a warning glint.

The family meal was long and leisurely. Seated next to Nick at the gleaming mahogany table, Lauren ate sparingly and listened to the conversation going on around her with growing weariness. At first they all made conscious efforts to speak in English for her benefit, but gradually the lapses into their own language became more frequent. She could hardly find it in herself to blame them too much under the circumstances. Much of the talk concerned people and places outside her experience anyway.

Nick himself seemed content to stay on the fringe, answering when directly addressed but otherwise contributing little. He was almost equally out of place, Lauren decided, and he had to recognise that fact. At one point she caught his grandfather watching her with an odd expression on his features, and looked hastily away again, wondering if her thoughts had been showing too clearly. It wasn't really up to her to approve or disapprove of what Nick was doing—at least not in public. She owed him that much loyalty.

It was gone eleven before anyone made a move to adjourn to the salon. Lauren took the opportunity to plead fatigue from the journey, half relieved when Nick declined to join her immediately. It had been a day of some emotional strain. She needed time on her own to recover from it.

'Tomorrow we will spend together,' promised Donata warmly. 'The whole day!'

While Nick did what? Lauren wondered, murmuring an appropriate response. How he could even contemplate giving up the life he knew for this thankless existence she couldn't begin to imagine. His grandfather looked capable of living another twenty years, so he stood to be approaching sixty before he could count on taking his place. And what of her? Did he really believe she was going to stand by him all that time—or did he not care? The latter thought hurt more than she wanted to acknowledge.

She was in bed but still awake when he finally came in. He looked at her with lifted brows as she sat up.

'I thought you were tired.'

'I am,' she said. 'Tired of being taken for a fool! I won't stay here, Nick. Not on this footing.'

He remained where he was, leaning against the bedpost, his face austere in the lamplight. 'What footing is that?'

She drew in a shaky breath. 'You know what I'm talking about. You don't have the right to do what you're doing to your grandfather. Not when it could be avoided.'

'How?' The tone was still controlled.

She had practised it in her mind for the last hour, but it took a lot of saying. 'By forfeiting your claim in favour of Vincenzo. That way everybody would gain.'

There was no reading his expression. 'Vincenzo doesn't bear the name Severino either.'

'But he is pure Italian, and that's what your grandfather is really concerned about.'

'You know him so well already?'

'I understand him.' She could sense his growing anger yet refused to allow it to deter her. 'It isn't unreasonable to want what he wants. If you didn't hate him so much you'd see how totally unfair you're being. He's an old man who . . .'

'He's an old man who refused to speak one single direct word to my mother in almost thirty years.' The interruption was soft but deadly. 'Is that what you'd call reasonable too?'

Lauren was still as a statue, eyes dark with shock. 'It isn't possible!' she breathed, and wasn't aware she had spoken aloud until she saw Nick's expression.

'Are you calling me a liar?' he demanded.

'No, of course not.' She paused in confusion, realising that was what she had implied. 'I just can't imagine anyone doing a thing like that. Why did he persuade her to leave your father and come back to Venice if he felt so strongly?'

'I already told you. He had a commitment towards continuing the line of inheritance, regardless of the way he felt.' Each word was clipped and harsh. 'I spent those eight months while my father fought for custody in sheer misery because I could see what it was doing to my mother to live with his silence. She'd come back believing he'd forgiven her, but he isn't a forgiving man.'

'Neither are you,' Lauren said softly. Her eyes were fixed on his face, willing him to listen. 'Is it worth ruining your whole life just to get even?'

His laugh jarred. 'You haven't seen a fraction of what I stand to inherit yet.'

'You may be too old to enjoy it by the time you do.'

'That's a risk I'll have to take.'

Lauren watched him helplessly as he moved away from the post, fingers loosening his tie as he went.

There was no getting through to him. He had lived too long with this desire for revenge. Thinking about it, she could appreciate his motives, yet that didn't make things any better.

'What about me?' she demanded. 'I meant what I said. I can't live this way!'

'You'll learn.' He sounded unmoved. 'You'll have to learn.'

'You can't make me stay!'

He looked at her then, taking in the tumbled red-gold hair and finely moulded features, the smooth bareness of her shoulders. Something flickered deep down in his eyes. 'I'll make you a proposition,' he said. 'If you still want to leave in the morning I'll take you to the airport and put you on the first available flight to Heathrow.'

'I have a better idea.' She was throwing back the cover as she spoke, forcing her limbs into movement. 'I'll go tonight!'

Nick dropped the shirt he had just taken off on the floor and came after her, catching her about the waist to swing her back on to the bed and following her down to pin her beneath him. Lauren fought back savagely until he caught both wrists and locked them above her head, hating him and wanting him at one and the same time. Then he was kissing her and she was kissing him back, anger dissolving at the touch of his hands on her skin, body hungrily reaching. They came together with the ease of familiarity, moving to a rhythm growing steadily faster and fiercer until all sense of time and place vanished and they were floating in free fall from a thousand feet.

'Not tonight,' Nick said roughly when breath returned. 'Not tomorrow either. If it isn't love, it's a good enough substitute.'

Whatever it was, it had her trapped, acknowledged

Lauren with fatalistic acceptance. But that didn't mean she was finished. If she could find a way to rid Nick of this obsession they might stand a chance of making their marriage work. She had to find a way!

Donata's plans for the day meant a start right after breakfast. Guido was waiting for them below. Getting into the gondola, Lauren noted that the motor launch was also tied up to the landing stage in readiness.

'Vincenzo is to take Nicholas to Murano,' said Donata, following her glance. 'The di Severinos have been involved in the glass industry a comparatively short time, and the name itself is not used, but it is a valuable source of income to the Estate. The family also owns a great deal of property both here in Venice itself and on the mainland, and then there are the vineyards in the Veneto. You see, there is a lot for Nicholas to learn.'

'While Vincenzo has been steeped in it since childhood,' murmured Lauren, and drew a sharp glance.

'That is not what I meant to imply.'

'I know.' Lauren smiled at the Italian girl. 'I was just thinking out loud.' She made a small sound of appreciation as the gondola passed out beneath the stone arch into the bright warm daylight of the canal, seeing the reflection of the building from which they had just emerged ripple like a mirage as their passage disturbed the water's surface. 'How peaceful!'

'Wait until we turn into the Grande,' said Donata. There was a pause before she added quietly, 'Do you not favour the idea of living here in Venice, Lauren?'

'Frankly, no.' Lauren saw no reason to disguise her feelings on that score. 'It's very beautiful, but. . . .' She lifted her shoulders wryly.

'But it is not home,' Donata finished for her with understanding. 'I would feel that way myself should I be asked to live elsewhere, but it is a sacrifice wives must often be forced to make, I think. Is Nicholas not worth it?'

'I didn't know about all this until after we were married,' Lauren evaded.

'You mean you would not have married him had you known? But if you love him. . . .' Donata paused again, tone altering a little. 'You do love him?'

Lauren still wasn't sure if love was the right word to describe what she felt for Nick, but there was no way she was going to reveal her doubts. 'I just don't happen to believe it's a wife's place to accept everything thrown at her simply because she is a wife.' She stole a sideways glance at the girl seated beside her. 'Don't you feel your brother is more entitled to inherit?'

The smooth olive-skinned brow drew into a faint frown. 'Vincenzo is not of direct descent.'

'That wasn't the question I asked.'

Donata sighed. 'It is a very difficult question to answer. What I feel and what I know is right are two different matters. All his life Vincenzo has known that one day Nicholas will return to claim his birthright. He would have been foolish to hope that it would not happen that way.'

'And Fiorella?' Lauren asked slyly. 'Was he foolish to allow himself to fall in love with a girl already promised to another man?'

Donata gave her a startled look. 'You knew about that?'

'Only by putting two and two together. She's free to marry anyone she wants now, isn't she?'

'Not in the way you mean. In spite of our family connections with the di Severino name, Vincenzo would not be considered suitable.'

'Yet Nick was and he isn't even pure Italian.'

'Ah, but Nicholas was an exception to the rule. It is not generally considered his fault that his mother chose to marry an Englishman.'

'Except by his grandfather.'

'Perhaps.' Donata sighed again. 'Zio Vittore is a much embittered man.'

They were coming out into the Grand Canal, catching the wash from a tourist boat as Guido back-poled to avoid being run down. Lauren clutched the side of the gondola as they rocked, relaxing only when they were safely in mid-canal and out of the path of the larger vessels, for the moment at least. The sun was already high, its heat scorching her bare arms. She was grateful for the shade of the canopy overhead. Sunstroke was the last thing she needed.

As before, the sheer variety of architecture bemused her. Every window, it seemed, had a different design, every rooftop a different level. In the distance could be seen towers and domes, silhouetted against the clean-washed sky. It was a hundred paintings come to life.

She recognised the symmetrical arches of the Rialto bridge as they rounded the final bend into the busy concourse. The vaporettos appeared to be everywhere, causing Guido to weave his craft skilfully between them to a small landing-stage on the right-hand side of the Canal. Lauren was glad of his assistance to climb out of the gondola, her legs trembling a little as she took her first steps on dry land.

'You will soon become accustomed to it,' commented Donata smilingly, noting her shakiness. 'Now we walk. Guido will meet us later at the Piazetta.'

The market place lined both sides of the alleyway leading from the bridge, the crowds so thick it was difficult to pick a way through without bumping into someone. Donata tucked a hand beneath Lauren's arm in order to keep the two of them together, ignoring the many stalls packed with an inviting array of goods.

'There will be another time for the markets after we do as Nicholas asked,' she said on the one occasion when Lauren suggested pausing for a moment to look at some leather handbags. 'Those are for tourists.'

Lauren gave in with good grace. It was Donata's day. In the next few minutes she lost all sense of direction as they twisted and turned from one narrow alley into another, passing shop windows bearing every imaginable kind of merchandise. Their destination lay off the main thoroughfares, squeezed in between a chemist and a jeweller's, its small window displaying a single dress in creamy white chiffon hung against a background of black velvet.

Inside they were greeted in voluble Italian by a slender and exquisitely dressed woman whose streaked blonde hair was fastened into a smooth chignon. Donata introduced her as Signora Fettorini. It was a different world, the carpets thick and springy underfoot, the decor all mirror glass and silk hangings. There wasn't a garment in sight.

The Signora whisked the two of them through into a smaller room totally lined with mirrors and furnished with a couple of gilt chairs, inviting them to take seats while she went to make arrangements. A few minutes later a rack full of clothing was wheeled into the dressing-room, with Signora Fettorini following on behind.

'Now,' she said. 'We shall begin!'

Two hours later, Lauren was the owner of a bewilderingly large new wardrobe, every item of which both Donata and Signora Fettorini swore she needed.

'It will be expected for the wife of *Il Signor* to set

fashions in dress,' claimed the former firmly when Signora Fettorini had departed to supervise the packing and despatch of the new garments. 'Nicholas recognises that need if you do not.'

'*Il Signor?*' Lauren queried. 'I thought that meant The Lord or something similar?'

'Or the Owner.' Donata shrugged. 'It is the same.'

'But premature, surely? Your great-uncle looks good for many years yet.'

It was Donata's turn to look surprised. 'Nicholas has not told you?'

Something tautened ominously in Lauren's chest. 'Told me what?'

'That Zio Vittore has only a short time to live—a matter of weeks perhaps.' Her face was sad. 'He has a rare disease which attacks the blood. There is nothing more that medicine can do.'

Lauren was silent, her mind grappling with this new development. Only yesterday Nick had told her he knew of no reason why his grandfather shouldn't live another twenty years or more, but in that case why choose now of all times to claim his inheritance? Coincidence? She doubted it. Even his marriage to her was probably part of his overall plan. The dying man was to be allowed no comfort.

'He didn't tell me,' she said grimly.

Donata made a small sound of distress. 'And now I have—how do you say it—let the kittens out of the bag!'

'Cat,' Lauren corrected automatically. She forced a smile. 'Don't worry about it.'

'Nicholas must have had good reason,' insisted the other.

Oh, yes, Lauren thought. Very good reason! He had known what her reaction would be. She looked at the simple honey-coloured silk suit she had chosen to keep on, controlling the desire to rip it off again with an effort. The clothes were only a minor part of this affair. Nick had far more to answer for!

'Don't worry about it,' she repeated, striving for a lighter note. 'I suppose he wanted to break me in to the idea gradually. After all, marriage itself is enough to be going on with.'

'Of course.' Donata was obviously relieved by her change of attitude. She looked at her watch. 'We have no time before luncheon to choose the rest of the things you will need. They must wait until we have eaten.'

Lauren wasn't hungry, but didn't like to upset Donata's plans. A cup of coffee wouldn't hurt her anyway. It might even help to steady her churned-up emotions.

The restaurant had an open patio overlooking one of the quiet side canals, the overhanging trees providing shade. At the far end, close by the water, a pair of tables had been pushed together to seat eight people. The six already seated were all young and of mixed sexes, their chatter and laughter clearly audible across the width of the patio. It wasn't until one of them turned round and lifted a hand in smiling greeting, that Lauren realised she and Donata were to make up the party.

Introductions were casual, by first name only. Seated between Donata and one of the young men Lauren listened to the fast-flowing exchanges around the table and wondered wryly if she would ever be able to understand a fraction of what was being said. Providing she even stayed, of course, she reflected at that point, recalling what she had learned. Nick was using her in more ways than one. She had every excuse for leaving him. If only the thought of doing just that didn't hurt quite so much.

The afternoon was drawing into evening by the time they joined Guido at the end of the Piazetta, the western sky already heralding the blood red of sunset. The crowds had thinned, leaving the waterfront clear of all but a few strollers. Accustomed by now to the motion of the gondola, Lauren lay relaxed in her seat and viewed the passing scene, seeing the shadows deepen, the water's surface turn to ebony, the lights begin to spring behind the iron grilles of countless windows. The noise and bustle of the day were past and gone, the peace returned. It was a contrast she could appreciate.

Donata's mother was descending the stairs as the two girls came up from below.

'You have had a good day?' she inquired, pausing in her step.

It was Lauren who answered, her smile polite. 'Very, thank you. I have enough clothes for several people, and to cover every possible occasion.'

'Except perhaps your wedding,' came the smooth reply. 'It is to take place in the chapel at Rivago one week from tomorrow. That means we must all of us be ready to travel the very next day after the Ball in order to prepare. Naturally, your father will be expected to lend his presence to the occasion. You will contact him?'

'I have to do that anyway,' said Lauren, not at all sure how to react to the news. 'He doesn't even know where I am.'

There was no way of telling if her slip had been noted. The Signora's expression did not alter. 'Then now would be a good time. There is a telephone in your room.'

'I noticed.' Lauren hesitated, searching the older woman's features. 'Are you in agreement?'

'Zio Vittore wishes it this way.' The statement held flat finality. 'A civil marriage has no real meaning for him.'

And Il Signore's word was law, thought Lauren wryly. 'Is Nick back yet?' she asked, shelving the whole issue for the moment.

Cristina Laurentiis shook her head. 'They had much to do. Nicholas has wasted so much time.'

Donata had gone on ahead. Following, Lauren tried to work out in her mind what she was going to say to Nick when he did return—what she was going to do after she had said it. Leaving him was no real solution, even if he would let her go, because they would still be legally tied, yet to simply go along with his plans for the future was beyond her too. She wasn't even sure for how long she could expect to share in them anyway. He wanted her now, but physical desire had a way of burning itself out when there was no other emotion backing it up.

She caught up with Donata along the corridor which led to both their rooms, shaking her head to the other's questioning glance.

'I just wanted to ask you about this Ball your mother spoke of. Is it in aid of something special?'

'It is to celebrate the official announcement of my betrothal,' Donata acknowledged. 'It will be a double celebration now, of course.'

'Oh, but that's unfair!' Lauren protested. 'It should be your night, and yours alone!'

The Italian girl smiled. 'I have no objection to sharing the occasion. Filippo will be flattered to stand alongside you and Nicholas in the receiving line. The name of Camon will benefit from the association. The blue gown we purchased from Signora Fettorini will be eminently suitable. She will be distraught not to have more time in which to prepare your wedding gown.'

'I shan't want anything special,' Lauren responded swiftly. 'It isn't as if we're being married for the first time.'

'In Zio Vittore's eyes it will be the first time.' Donata lifted delicate shoulders. 'It is for you to decide. Your father will be here?'

'I hope so.' Lauren could find no further excuse to put off the moment she dreaded. 'I'm going to phone him right now.'

It took courage to lift the telephone receiver in the bedroom, and even more determination to hold on to it while the connection was being made. Carol answered the call, her business-like tone vanishing as soon as Lauren spoke.

'Thank heaven you called! Your father has been going frantic trying to trace you. Where are you?'

'The Palazzo Ambrogio,' Lauren told her, anticipating the sudden intake of breath on the other end of the line. 'It's a long story, Carol. I'd rather wait to see you before I tell it.' She paused. 'Is Dad in?'

'Yes.' The other wasted no more time. 'I'm putting you through.'

Hugh Devlin sounded agitated when he spoke. 'Lauren, we've been worried about you! What on earth possessed you to go marrying a man who could do what he did?'

What indeed? Lauren took a grip on herself. 'It was a misunderstanding,' she said. 'Mostly my own fault.'

'Mostly my fault,' he corrected ruefully. 'If I hadn't. . . .' He caught himself up, obviously recognising the futility in self-accusation. 'Darling, you didn't have to marry the man just because you'd been to bed with him.'

'I know,' she said. 'And I didn't.'

'You mean you fell in love with him?'

Right up until that moment Lauren had intended answering that particular question with an affirmative simply because it was the easiest way out. Now, actually faced with it, she found herself hesitating just a fraction too long. 'It's difficult to explain,' she got out at last. 'If falling in love means being totally bowled over, then that's what happened.'

'Only now you're able to see straight again and it isn't the same?'

'Something like that.' She added resignedly, 'It's impossible to explain things over the phone. It's all too complicated. Dad, his family want us to marry again in church. I'd like you to be there. Is it possible for you to come here to Venice yourself?—you *and* Carol preferably.'

'I'll make it possible.' There was a pause and a change of tone, 'I checked the Clayfield account yesterday. . . .'

'Nick took care of it,' she said. 'You owe him the money when you get it.' She was too churned up inside to carry on the conversation much longer. 'How soon can you be here?'

'Tuesday,' came the decisive reply. 'I'll get Carol to book a flight as soon as I get off the phone. And Lauren, if you're not happy with things the way they are you're coming right back home with us, husband or no husband! All right?'

'All right.' There was no other answer she could make. 'Let me know your flight number and I'll arrange to meet you at the Customs' terminal.'

Nick came into the room as she replaced the receiver, one hand going up automatically to loosen the constricting tie as he closed the door.

'Who was that?' he asked.

'My father.' She kept her voice carefully expression-less. 'I was asked to get him here in time for the wedding next weekend.'

'So soon?' He had moved across to start emptying his pockets at the dressing table, his back to her. 'The old devil doesn't waste any time!'

'Stop calling him that!' Lauren drew in a tremulous breath, steadying her nerves. 'Why didn't you tell me he was dying?'

# CHAPTER EIGHT

NICK seemed to be a long time finding a reply, his fingers separating the items deposited as if checking that nothing was missing. 'Who told you that?' he asked at length. There was no trace of emotion in his voice.

'Donata.' She waited, lip curling when he neither moved nor spoke. 'You married me just to taunt him, didn't you? He couldn't even be allowed to die in peace!'

He turned then, gaze narrowed and steely. 'That's how you see it?'

'How else am I supposed to see it?' The tremor was in her voice now but the pain went too deep to allow for any backtracking. 'And don't try pleading justification either. He may have been instrumental in your mother's decision to leave your father, but it was her own choice to stay.'

His smile was without humour. 'I don't suppose it occurred to you to ask me first if I knew he was dying?'

Lauren stared at him, totally at a loss. 'You had to have known,' she stammered. 'Donata didn't give me the impression it was any secret.'

'Possibly because she took it for granted that Vincenzo would have passed on the information.'

'But he didn't?'

'No, he didn't. Nor did anyone else.' He lifted his shoulders in an expressive shrug at the doubt in her face. 'Ask if you don't believe me.'

'But why?' Lauren was bewildered. 'They must have realised you'd have come back earlier if you'd known.'

'That may be the reason. The longer I stayed away, the greater the hope for Vincenzo's future. I'm grateful to them for keeping it from me this long. There was a chance I might have felt pressured into marrying Fiorella Bianchi regardless if I'd known before.'

'To satisfy a man you hate?'

'Who can continue to hate the dying?' There was a rueful note to his voice. 'I wanted to see him suffer, but not this way.'

Lauren sat looking at him for a long moment before rising unsteadily to her feet, crossing to where he stood to put both hands to his face and reach for his lips. 'I misjudged you,' she said humbly. 'I'm sorry, Nick.'

His arms came roughly about her, pulling her against him and holding her there. His mouth was searching, rousing her to passion with a speed and immediacy that made her tremble. Without conscious prompting, her fingers slipped open the buttons of his shirt, baring the dark curls of hair to her exploration, her nostrils filling with the emotive male scent of him, her hips beginning to move in the slow concentric circles he himself had taught her to employ, feeling his response.

They made love right there in the thick pile of the carpet, their clothing discarded around them, discretion thrown to the winds. Afterwards it seemed natural to stay where they were, wrapped together like Siamese twins while the heartbeats steadied and peace stole over them. When Nick did finally stir it was with reluctance.

'I must be getting old,' he said, 'but I can't stand the draught down here! Don't you feel it?'

Lauren chuckled, looking up into the lean face with laughter sparking her eyes. 'I have a blanket.'

Grey eyes sprang a glint of their own. Holding her by the arms, he rolled over on to his back, bringing her on top of him. 'Not any more!'

He was right, there was a draught, albeit a warm one. She laughed again and kissed him, then pushed herself to her feet, lifting both hands in an instinctive and totally feminine gesture to pat her hair into some semblance of order.

'Like a cat,' he said softly, regaining his own feet. 'The grooming is all-important!' He reached for her again, hands drifting possessively over her body, his smile tantalising as he watched her reaction. 'I always envied the female recovery rate!'

Lauren closed her eyes, leaning contentedly against him. If this wasn't love it was something she could live with. Many had started with less.

'When will you tell him?' she murmured, allowing her own hands to drift in the same desultory fashion.

'Tell him what?' he asked.

'That you've changed your mind.' She was smiling, recognising the stirring of response. Female recovery rate indeed! It took the silence and sudden stillness in him to bring her down to earth. Eyes opened and questioning, she looked up at him, meeting a gaze gone brittle again. 'You have changed your mind, haven't you?'

'If you mean am I going to hand over everything to Vincenzo, the answer is no,' he said. 'I'll simply have to make the necessary adjustments faster than I anticipated.'

'But you said you didn't hate your grandfather any more!'

'I said I couldn't go on hating a dying man. That doesn't mean I'm willing to indulge him all the way.'

The tremor that ran through her had nothing to do with prior emotions. She drew away from him blindly, his very touch suddenly anathema to her. 'I was right that very first day,' she whispered. 'You are a bastard, Nick!'

'Because I won't do what you think I should do?' He shook his head, mouth grimly set. 'You can make me want you the way I never wanted any woman before, Lauren, but there's no way you're going to rule my life for me!'

She said it with bitterness, 'Want is the only word you know!'

'You'd call what you feel by a different name?'

A few minutes ago the answer would have been yes, she thought numbly. But a few minutes ago she had been with another man. 'I don't know what I'd call it,' she retorted. 'I only know I'm ashamed of it.'

His laugh jarred. 'That might sound convincing if I didn't have a good memory for detail. You weren't ashamed of what you were doing just now.' There was nothing loverlike in the glance he ran over her. 'You'd better get some clothes on while the going, as they say, is good. I'd hate to undermine your principles any further.'

Lauren bit her lip as he turned away, unable to ignore the leaping of her pulses at the fluid ripple of muscle beneath taut, tanned skin. They were as far apart as ever in every way that really mattered, with little hope of reaching agreement. What she had to decide was whether what they had was going to be enough.

Filippo Camon took dinner with the family on the Sunday evening. He was a young man of some twenty-six or -seven years, attractive to look at but rather too straight-faced for Lauren's tastes. With Nick one could at least share a joke. She had a feeling that Donata's betrothed rarely laughed out loud.

She watched the pair of them together in the salon after the meal, seeing little sign of emotion on either side. A marriage of expediency, she decided. Arranged by Il Signore, no doubt. Yet Donata seemed happy enough on the surface. Whether she was or she wasn't, it was none of her affair, she told herself firmly at that point. Leave well alone. She had enough problems on her own plate.

Nick hadn't touched her in two whole days, although his manner towards her in public, as of now, was always exemplary. She was probably the only one who noted the cynical twist to his lips whenever he glanced in her direction, the slight hardening of inflection when he spoke to her. There had been more than one time when she had yearned to tell him she didn't care what he did regarding his future position, except that it wouldn't have been wholly true. The thought of spending her life following the same seemingly aimless pattern of existence that Donata and her mother did was no encouragement. Despite the changes in the outside world, tradition still lived on in this household. Only with the passing of the patriarch might the old values start to crumble, and even then not overnight.

With hindsight, it was easy to perceive that the old man was ill. His sallow skin and lacklustre eyes, his general lethargy—all pointed in the same direction. Apart from that one interview in the library the first afternoon, Lauren had seen him only at dinner. She supposed that gradually he would retire more and more to his own quarters as weakness overcame him. He was too proud a man to let others see him slowly fade away.

He had been sitting quietly listening to the general conversation for the past few minutes. Now, as if sensing Lauren's thoughts, he looked across at her. 'Come, sit by me,' he said. 'We have had little opportunity to speak together since you arrived.'

Lauren obeyed the injunction, aware of Nick's sharp

glance. The dark eyes were not lacking in shrewdness as they studied her face.

'Tell me how you and Nicholas met,' he said. 'It cannot have been so long ago.'

'It was at my father's office,' she answered with truth. 'He was coming out as I was waiting to go in.' She knew Nick was listening; some devil in her promoted the addition. 'One look was enough for both of us!'

From the slant of his lips, Signor di Severino was not wholly deceived. 'So why did you marry in Rome and in such haste? Did your father not approve?'

'He didn't know,' Lauren was forced to admit, wishing Nick would come to her aid. 'It . . . happened unexpectedly.'

Enlightenment dawned. 'Ah, I see, It was to be just another affair until this grandson of mine realised what he had found!'

Nick was wearing a cynical smile of his own. 'You make me sound like Casanova himself! Lauren is a different matter. She always was. I married her before she could change her mind, that's all.'

White brows lifted enquiringly in her direction. 'You had doubts?'

Lauren glanced swiftly at Nick and away again, receiving no help. 'Some,' she acknowledged cautiously.

'But not now?'

There was only one way she could answer that question. She did so with head high and voice quite steady. 'No.'

'It is good to be certain of one's emotions,' came the ironical comment. 'Your true love will see you both through the difficult times ahead.'

Would lust? Lauren wondered, struggling to maintain a certain composure beneath the concerted gazes of both men. Nick must be laughing up his sleeve at her discomfiture.

Her pride underwent a further test when he turned his back on her again that night in their bed. She had to force herself to break the silence between them.

'I don't see much point in getting my father out here to attend a wedding that isn't going to take place,' she said into the darkness. 'I want to go home, Nick.'

It was a moment or two before he replied, although she could tell from his breathing that he wasn't asleep. 'I can't stop you,' he said at last. 'It has to be your decision.'

It wasn't what she had wanted to hear, Lauren acknowledged in a burst of honesty. She had hoped he would try to dissuade her. When she spoke again her voice sounded small and shaky. 'Don't you even want me any more?'

He sighed then, rolling over on to his back to lie gazing at the ornate ceiling. 'Yes, I want you,' he said. 'I'm just tired of the censure. Marrying you without telling you my background first was a mistake, I'll admit that. I should have taken a chance.'

Would it have made any real difference at the time? Lauren wondered, recalling her blind aquiescence. In fact, it might very well have added to the romance of the moment. One had to be here inside the situation to realise its full potential.

'It's such a different world,' she said. 'Almost archaic!'

'Then stay and help me change it.'

She rolled her head to look at him, seeing the jut of the firm profile still upturned. 'Is that what you plan to do?'

'Gradually, yes. There'd be no arranged marriages for our children, you could be sure!'

Our children. The very thought made her feel all churned up inside. If love could grow between two people it was very possible that a child might speed the process. The question was hesitant. 'You won't consider changing your mind?'

'I can't.' The statement came without equivocation. 'Right or wrong, my mother sacrificed everything to the one end. If I turn my back on that fact it makes everything she did worthless.'

It was Lauren's turn to sigh. 'I hadn't looked at it like that before.' She paused, knowing the reply she was going to make yet still reluctant to commit herself. 'All right, Nick, I'll stay.'

He came to her then, pulling her roughly into his arms. 'You won't regret it,' he promised.

With his mouth on hers she could find no room for any emotion beyond desire. Like putty in his hands, a small, fading part of her mind accused her, but she turned a deaf ear. Time would alter many things, their depth of feeling included. Who could fail to love a man who could give such exquisite pleasure as this!

Hugh Devlin arrived alone on the Tuesday afternoon. Carol sent her love, he said, but someone had to stay and look after things at the office.

'I'm still not sure what to think about all this,' he admitted, holding Lauren away from him to look at her after their initial greeting. His eyes searched her face. 'Are you happy?'

She nodded, ignoring the small shaft of doubt. 'You wouldn't be here if I wasn't. It's going to be a busy few days. Thursday night is the Grand Ball, then on Friday afternoon we all of us travel to Rivaga in the Veneto for the ceremony on Saturday. When do you have to go back?'

'Sunday.' He wasn't yet wholly convinced. 'You

know,' he added, 'it's taking some getting used to. You only left home a week ago.'

'I know.' She kept her tone level. 'I'm sorry for the deception too. I hope you didn't blame Carol for not telling you sooner.'

'I did,' he acknowledged wryly, 'but we got over it. You shouldn't have done it, Lauren. I'd rather have gone to jail than have you demean yourself that way!'

'But everything worked out for the best,' she rejoined swiftly. Guido had gone on ahead with the single suitcase. Lauren took her father's arm as they followed along the quayside. 'Dad, you won't let it come between you and Nick when you meet, will you? I want the two of you to be friends.'

The answering smile was dry. 'That's a tall order when it concerns the man who took my daughter for his mistress.'

'It wasn't wholly his fault.' Lauren defended. 'I gave him the wrong impression in the first place.'

'It's no excuse, but for your sake I'll try to put it behind me.' The irony increased. 'After all, I'm in no position to start casting stones! I still owe the man a lot of money.'

There was nothing she could say to that. She didn't even try. Guido was waiting at the boat, face impassive as ever. Hugh gave the livery another bemused glance, but made no comment, stepping down gingerly into the gently rocking craft in Lauren's wake and taking a seat at her side.

'You look as if you've been doing this all your life,' he said as they got under way. 'I knew Nick Brent was half Italian, but I don't think anyone realised just what kind of background he came from.'

'Wait till you see the Palazzo,' Lauren warned. 'It's pure Renaissance!'

'And Nick owns it?'

'Not yet.' She bit her lip, remembering how much she still had to tell him and wondering how and when to start. Not here and now for sure. Guido might have little to say for himself, but he probably understood English as well as the majority of Italians she had so far come into contact with. 'We'll talk later,' she added. 'Nick won't be home until around six. He's out with the son of the family comptroller. The Laurentiis live at the Palazzo too. You'll meet them all at dinner.'

'That should prove interesting.' He was looking at the scenery, glance lingering on the large square, triple-balconied façade just coming up on their right. 'Palazzo Corner della Ca'Grande,' he murmured. 'I remember most of the names, including the Ambrogia, although it never occurred to me all those years ago that there might come a time when I'd be visiting on a personal basis!'

'You've been to Venice before?' Lauren asked, surprised. 'I never knew that.'

'No reason why you should. It was before you were born. Your mother and I spent our honeymoon here.' He was smiling at the memory. 'Italy has always been one of my favourite countries. I knew it fairly well in my teens and early twenties.'

'Can you speak the language at all?'

'I used to be able to. Can't say I've had much call to practice it these last twenty years or so.' He glanced at her, the smile still there. 'Let's see now ... *erano secoli che non ti vedevo*. Literally translated, that means I haven't seen you for centuries, which is what it felt like. I expect I'm going to have to accustom myself to missing you.'

'I'll miss you too.' There was a lump in her throat.

'I'm glad you've got Carol, Dad. It would have made things perfect if she could have been here with you.'

'She'll come next time,' he promised.

The Palazzo left him speechless. Lauren took him straight up to the room which had been prepared for him, closing the door before launching herself into the speech she had been preparing for days. Her father listened without interruption until she had finished, shaking a bemused head.

'I keep getting the feeling I'm going to waken up in a minute or two and find this is all a dream!'

Lauren had known that same feeling on more than one occasion. 'It's no dream,' she said. 'It's only too real.'

'Mistress of this place!' His tone was ironic. 'Odd the different connotations that same word can take on.' He looked at her searchingly. 'How do you feel about it? Really feel about it, I mean.'

'Nervous,' she admitted.

'But Nick makes it all worth while?'

'Yes.' The answer was too quick and too assertive, and she knew her father had noted it. She made haste to add, 'I'm learning to adapt.'

'Nick too?' he asked.

Lauren smiled and lifted her shoulders. 'It's not his problem. There'll be some tea in the small salon in about fifteen minutes, if you want to come down: a special concession to English habits. Otherwise, you can have it up here. You'll be meeting everyone at dinner anyway.'

'I'll come down,' he said. 'Dinner sounds as if it might be a bit overwhelming.'

The room Lauren shared with Nick was just along the next corridor. After a swift shower, she got into a simple but effective little dress in navy blue with white piping around the collar, sliding her feet into matching high-heeled sandals. Changing for the said afternoon tea had become a ritual. Signora Laurentiis set high store by appearances. Lauren didn't mind indulging her. The climate alone provided incentive enough, although she was gradually growing accustomed to the heat outside. Here in the Palazzo itself it was always cool. In the winter there would be fires in the great hearths. She didn't want to think that far ahead. One day at a time had become her maxim.

The Signora was already presiding over the silver tea kettle when father and daughter arrived, Donata close by. Lauren performed introductions, pleased and proud when her father addressed his hostess in what sounded to her ears like fluent Italian. After a week she could just about work out the gist of what he was saying, stifling a giggle at the thought of Carol's reactions to the same flowery compliments.

'Don't mind me,' she told them some minutes later when Cristina apologised for carrying on the conversation in the same language. 'It's time I started really trying.'

The older woman looked delighted. 'Zio Vittore would be enchanted!' she exclaimed. 'Tonight at dinner we will all converse in Italian. No one will mind if you make mistakes. Your own papa can correct you.'

'I'm rusty myself,' protested the latter good-humouredly. 'You'll probably have to correct us both!'

'We will all help,' declared Donata. She was laughing, her whole face lit with anticipation. 'It will be fun!'

'You seem to be having a good time,' remarked Nick from the doorway. He was smiling too, the eyes meeting those of the man even now rising to greet him untouched by any hint of constraint. 'Glad you could get here in time for the wedding. Lauren would have been disappointed.'

'I wouldn't have wanted to miss it,' acknowledged the older man. It was an obvious effort to act naturally with someone he had last seen in such different circumstances; obvious to Lauren at least. 'I'm afraid I shan't have a partner though. Carol stayed behind to keep things ticking over while I'm away.'

Nick shrugged. 'You should have said. I could have made arrangements.'

So he hadn't done anything yet about severing his connections with the business, Lauren reflected. She had wondered about that, yet hadn't liked broaching the subject. Their emotional relationship was still too precariously balanced to take any strain. For now she had to be content to let things lie.

'You're early,' she remarked on a bright note. 'That's nice! Is Vincenzo coming?'

'Vincenzo has no taste for tea,' said his mother, almost as if apologising for the fact. Her hand hovered over the kettle. 'Nicholas, you will take a cup?'

'Why not?' He sounded easy. 'I can think of worse ways of spending half an hour.'

Lauren was seated beside her father on one of the gilt sofas. Nick took a chair on his own, stretching a hand to accept the delicate china then settling back against the brocade upholstery. He looked anything but comfortable, Lauren thought. His long, lean frame was made for lounging on a chesterfield with his feet up.

She had a sudden vision of him doing just that, clad in casual slacks and a roll-necked sweater, a book in hand and a couple of dogs sprawled on the rug beside him. Swiftly her imagination built the house around him: old and cottage, somewhere in the countryside, not too far from London. There was a blazing log fire in the open hearth and snowflakes falling outside the window, a delicious smell of cooking in the air causing him to lift his head and sniff appreciatively. He was getting up now and coming through into the low-ceilinged farmhouse kitchen where she stood at the Aga, sliding his hands about her waist to peer over her shoulder into the dish she was stirring, his breath warm on her cheek, his body subtly pressuring; he was taking the spoon from her hands and turning her towards him, kissing her with love and growing need until the distant cry of the baby in its cot upstairs broke them reluctantly apart. . . .

'Lauren?' Cristina's tone was quizzical. 'I asked you two times already if you would like more tea!'

Lauren came back to earth with a start, her gesture apologetic. 'I'm sorry. I was miles away! Yes please, I would.'

Both her father and Nick were looking at her, the former with amusement the latter with an expression she found singularly disturbing. One thing he couldn't command was her daydreams, she told herself defensively. They were hers to cherish, hopeless though they might be.

Dinner that evening was something of a trial for Lauren, although the sight and sound of her father conversing with ever-growing confidence was some consolation. Signor di Severino contributed little himself, but listened with obvious approval to his houseguest's efforts. Only on the occasions when his glance came to rest on either Nick or Lauren did his expression cloud at all.

Lauren wished it were only possible to grant him peace of mind, but Nick was not to be persuaded. He was wrong, and deep down he must know it, yet he intended to go ahead regardless. There was an alternative, and one she had at times considered over the past couple of days. She had no idea of the rules governing divorce here in Italy, but if Nick had been right about money easing the way to a quick marriage then it could very probably do the same towards dissolving it. Even if Fiorella Bianchi didn't answer his needs in a wife, there must be many other Italian girls who could. If she could only bring herself to view that prospect objectively it would provide the best solution. What use was there in being dog-in-the-manger over a man she neither loved nor was loved by?

She was still pondering that question when she was preparing for bed later on, watching Nick undress through the mirror as she brushed her hair. He was superbly built, there was no doubt, his back tapering from broad shoulders to narrow waist and hips, his buttocks firmly moulded above the long, muscular thighs. He was hairy only at the front, his skin smooth and blemish-free and permanently tanned. Just looking at him she could feel her senses heightening, the drumbeats beginning to throb in her ears.

Turning to stretch a hand for the bottom half of his dark silk pyjamas, he caught her eyes through the mirror. Lauren tore her gaze away and began brushing with more vigour, looking steadfastly at her own reflection yet unable to totally shut out the image behind her. He watched her for a long moment without moving, expression enigmatic as ever. Only when he began to come towards her could she see what was happening to him, the answering surge of heat sweeping through her from toe to tip, suspending the brush in mid-sweep as he loomed at her back.

He didn't speak, just took the hairbrush from her unresisting hand and tossed it lightly into a nearby chair, then slid his fingers along her bare shoulders to

ease down the thin straps of her nightdress. Her breasts
filled the palms of his hands, proudly uptilted, their
peaks rosy-tipped and enticing. He bent and brushed
aside her hair with his lips, planting tiny kisses from her
nape to her ear, nibbling gently at her lobe until she
could no longer contain the shuddering of her body.
The nightdress fell away from her as he lifted her from
the chair and into his arms, drifting unheeded to a
gossamer heap on the floor.

'I like your father,' he said a long time afterwards
when she lay with her head pillowed against his chest. 'I
never really met him before, except as an employee of
the firm. I'm glad it didn't come to a prosecution. He's
not the first man to give way to temptation of one kind
or another.'

There was something in his voice that Lauren
couldn't quite define. Softly, not wanting to spoil the
moment, she said, 'He knows he's lucky. He'll be only
too thankful to have the whole thing over and done
with.'

There was a pause before Nick spoke again. 'And
you?' he asked on a suddenly cynical note. 'Do you
think you're lucky?'

'Right now I do.' She rubbed her cheek against the
dark hair on his chest with a sigh of pure pleasure. 'I
feel fulfilled.'

'In one sense if not in another.'

Her sigh this time had a different sound. 'One can't
have everything, I suppose.'

'Apparently not.' The hand resting on the back of her
head had somehow hardened. 'We'll just have to make
the best of what we do have. Are you on the pill,
Lauren?'

The question took her by surprise, coming as it did
right out of the blue. 'I . . . well, yes,' she admitted. 'I

was hardly going to take any risks with the arrangement we had originally, was I?'

He didn't deny it. But there's no need to carry on with it now,' he said.

There was a dull pain deep inside her. 'You mean you want children right away?'

'The sooner the better.'

The better to seal his claim, she thought hollowly. The thought of bringing up a child of theirs here in what was and always would be to her a foreign country was not an enticing one, yet she couldn't disregard the part of her that wanted a child of Nick's either.

'So do I have your promise?' he asked after a moment or two. He sounded unwontedly harsh. 'You'll destroy them all?'

'Yes.' Any other answer would have destroyed any faint chance they might have of achieving something lasting from this marriage of theirs. 'You can do it for me, if you like.'

Something in him seemed to give a little. 'I trust your word.'

Trust alone was a step in the right direction, Lauren told herself comfortingly, feeling his hand smooth her hair. At this moment she could almost imagine that love already existed.

# CHAPTER NINE

Guests began arriving for the Ball from eight-thirty, some by water, some by land. Standing by Nick's side in the reception line in her beautiful but respectable dress of pale blue satin, Lauren wondered wryly what these same people would have made of her appearance at the last party she had attended. That was still only just over a week ago. It barely seemed possible. So much had happened since then; so much was still to happen. A couple of days from now she would walk down the aisle on her father's arm to marry the man who held her in thrall. Whatever freedom of choice she might have retained, it no longer applied.

Donata was wearing red, her dark hair piled gracefully high. She was smiling at someone speaking now to her and Filippo, but there was no real sparkle in her eyes. The date of her own wedding had been set for the end of the following month. It was to be a big Venetian society occasion right here in the city. Lauren wondered if Nick's grandfather would make it. He was here tonight but looking so drawn. Saturday was going to be a day of much sorrow for him. She hoped he could find it in himself to forgive the two of them for what they were doing to him before he died.

A sudden stirring among those in the immediate vicinity drew her eyes back towards the door and the latest arrivals. Nick had been laughing but a moment before, now he seemed struck dumb, his whole attitude stiffening. Three of the newcomers were total strangers, the fourth only too devastatingly familiar. Lauren gazed in numb dismay at the woman whose place she had taken, wondering what on earth Francesca was doing here at all, much less without her husband in tow. It had only been a week, and they hadn't been married long then. The man accompanying her had a facial resemblance to the older man with them, so it was possibly a family turnout. One thing seemed certain, they had little idea of the bombshell they were dropping.

Stefano Laurentiis looked as if he were hanging on to his composure by a thread as he greeted the party. Whether Signor di Severino also knew who Francesca was it was difficult to tell. His smiles were a rarity at the best of times.

From the manner in which people were glancing at Nick it was obvious that some were in possession of the facts. They were waiting to see what he would do when his former mistress reached him. Lauren was grateful that no one here knew of her previous meeting with the woman—but she had reckoned without Francesca herself on that score.

'I must address you as *Signora* tonight, must I not?' the latter remarked as she came level. There was malice in her smile as she looked from Lauren to Nick. 'I congratulate you. So much has happened since the last time we all of us met!'

Her companions were looking faintly bewildered. Lauren felt sorry for them because before the evening was out someone was certainly going to fill them in on the situation. The son's relationship with the lovely Roman was open to some speculation, although surely no man would inflict knowing embarrassment on his parents. Looking at him, Lauren felt fairly sure that he was unaware of Francesca's true background. It was only just beginning to dawn on him that some grave error of judgment had been committed.

Nick had himself well under control, the lean, handsome face giving little away. Lauren waited for him to ask where Luigi was, but he made no attempt. Had he known that the marriage was already on the rocks? she wondered as the party moved on to allow others to take their place. Anything was possible the way things were going. Yet if he had known, he certainly hadn't been expecting to see Francesca here tonight. That moment of stunned silence had been a genuine reaction.

The announcement of Donata and Filippo's impending nuptials was made before the supper break. Watching the former's face, Lauren sensed stoic submission behind the façade. Brother and sister were both of them caught in the same trap, conditioned from childhood to accept an order of things in which love played an insignificant part. Nick too might well have been the same had his father not regained control of his life. It was only thanks to the latter that she herself was where she was today, and she wasn't at all sure she should be grateful for that.

She had intended not to mention Francesca's presence until Nick brought up the subject himself, yet found her tongue overruling her head the first chance it had when she danced with him later.

'Did you know she was going to be here?' she demanded in low tones as they circled.

Nick made no attempt to play for time by asking who she was talking about. 'No,' he said.

'But you did know she'd left Luigi—always assuming that's what she has done?'

The face above her was without expression. 'I only heard a couple of days ago. And don't ask me how she managed to get herself asked here tonight because I've no idea. Francesca has many friends in many places.

She once told me she could arrange anything. Now I believe her.'

'Does she still attract you?' The question came without volition, drawing a faint satirical smile.

'If I said no, I'd be a liar. She always did attract me, she probably always will—until she loses her looks, of course.'

Lauren was silent for a moment before saying hardily, 'I won't have you coming to me from another woman, Nick!'

The grey eyes had a glitter. 'How would you know?'

'I'd know.' She drew in a shaky breath, fighting the urge to scream invective at him. 'You either promise me now that you won't see her again after tonight or we call off the ceremony altogether!'

The smile was still there but subtly altered in character, his gaze penetrating her soul. 'You'd really do that?'

She forced the word out. 'Yes.'

'Then you'd better get on with it.'

Lauren stared up at him, her heart suddenly heavy as lead. 'Is that what you want?'

'No, it isn't what I want. I just don't care for ultimatums.' His tone was level. 'We've shared many fine moments, *cara*. No doubt we'll share many more, given the opportunity. It's your choice. I can't hold you against your will.'

'But you won't give me your word?'

He shook his head. 'No.'

The music was slow and dreamy, the lights dimmed. In those following moments of indecision, Lauren became vitally aware of the hard male body against which she was held, remembering other moments of even greater closeness, of laughter and lightness, of gasping entreaty and overwhelming pleasure; of passion so fierce it could scarcely be contained. Did she want to give up all that? *Could* she give up all that?

But it wasn't only the physical aspect, she acknowledged in self-revelation. The very thought of not seeing Nick again, of never hearing his voice, was more than she could contemplate. Falling in love with a man incapable of any deep emotion was foolish, but she was doing it anyway. And it would take someone of greater strength of mind than she possessed to turn their back on even the faintest hope.

'You don't make any concessions, do you?' she said bitterly.

'You knew that when you married me,' he responded. His tone had softened a little. 'People don't change overnight. It takes time and patience. Forget about Francesca. She has nothing to do with the way we are together.'

A fact she could have accepted, Lauren told herself, were she only convinced that the other woman would stay in the past.

Vincenzo claimed her for the next dance, holding her very correctly and making polite conversation. It was cruel, and she knew it, yet there was a need in her to hurt someone, and Nick was inviolate.

'I suppose the Bianchis could hardly be invited considering the circumstances,' she said lightly during a lull. 'A pity though. I'd have liked to meet Fiorella, if only to see what Nick gave up.'

Her partner had stiffened at the mention of the name. Now, meeting over-bright green eyes, he gave a faint shrug. 'It was in deference to Signor Bianchi's own personal pride that the invitation was not extended, for no other reason. The arrangement was a private affair between the two families. It would have been made public only when the date for their marriage had been set.'

'Like Donata and Filippo?'

'Yes.' He looked at her with a certain appraisement. 'You do not understand these matters.'

'True,' Lauren acknowledged. 'Do you think your sister loves her husband-to-be?'

There was a pause before he replied. When he did so it was with patience. 'Filippo is a good man.'

'And very suitable.'

'That too.' His smile was slight. 'There are many Italian families which have not yet embraced the new order. Nicholas will no doubt bring changes enough in his time.'

'Would you?' she asked. 'I mean, if you were next in line would you want things to go on just the way they are now?'

'That is a futile question.'

'I know.' Her tone apologised for her. 'All the same. . . .'

'I am not sure,' he admitted at length. 'Perhaps not in every way.'

'And too late for Donata whatever happens.'

'There is little to be done about that. She accepts it.'

Lauren said seriously, 'Only because she doesn't have anyone to speak up for her. Your family name is Laurentiis not di Severino. Your uncle doesn't have any right to govern your every action!'

'He employs both my father and myself,' Vincenzo pointed out with indisputable logic. 'That gives him the right. You must not concern yourself with Donata's welfare, Lauren, She will be content enough.'

If contentment was enough then she supposed he was right. Perhaps in many ways, Donata would be happier than she was herself. She sighed suddenly. 'I spoke out of turn. Forgive me, Vincenzo.'

'There is nothing to forgive,' he denied. 'You cannot

be expected to appreciate our customs in so short a time.'

Lauren doubted if she would ever learn. No matter how long she lived here she would always be on the outside looking in.

There was no sign of Nick when they came off the floor. Unwilling to admit even to herself that she was equally concerned with finding Francesca, Lauren moved slowly through the crowded rooms. The Palazzo was built around a central courtyard, reached via steps descending at intervals from the covered balcony which stretched around three sides of the first floor. Finding the door leading from the music room standing slightly ajar, she went outside into the warm night, half expecting to see the two people she sought entwined in each other's arms, but instead finding only Donata.

'I was too hot,' explained the latter as she turned from her contemplation of the moon-shadowed court below. 'I needed some air.'

'Me too,' Lauren claimed lightly. 'Coincidental, isn't it, that we chose the same door!' She had closed the same as she came through, isolating the two of them from the noise inside. She leaned against the supporting pillar, the coolness of the stone pleasant against her skin. 'Won't Filippo be wondering where you got to?'

Donata's smile was faint. 'He knows I cannot be very far away.'

'In body, at least.'

A frown overcame the smile. 'I do not understand.'

'I mean,' Lauren said with deliberation, 'that your mind is free to go where it will.'

There was a pause while the two girls looked at one another. Donata was the first to break the silence.

'You are trying to ask me something, I think?'

Lauren hesitated only briefly. 'I suppose what I am asking is do you love Filippo?'

The answer came softly. 'You use the word as if it meant but one kind of emotion. I have a great respect for the man I am to marry—whose children I shall bear. That is of great importance.'

'But you don't yearn for his lovemaking?'

'I have never experienced it. How can I tell?' Donata spread her hands a little. 'You must realise that our ways are different. Filippo would never attempt to despoil his bride-to-be. Intimacy of that nature will take place for the first time on our wedding night.'

'When it's too late to change your mind.'

The smile was faint. 'There is more to a good marriage than the bedtime rituals. Filippo was chosen for me a long time ago. I see no cause to quarrel with that choice.'

'Does he feel the same sense of commitment?'

'To our marriage? Of course.'

'And to you personally?'

Donata shrugged. 'A man has certain needs one woman cannot fulfil.'

Lauren's laugh sounded just a little cracked. 'Oh, that I don't doubt! What you're saying is we shouldn't expect them to make any sacrifices.'

'No, that is not what I am saying.' Donata's tone was gentle, as if explaining to a child. 'It is a matter of what is the most important. The emotions shared by you and Nicholas are given only to a few. Be grateful.'

The laugh floating up from the courtyard below was light and feminine. Lauren stiffened, reading the same instant recognition in Donata's eyes. There was a moment of suspended animation before she moved, crossing on reluctant feet to the parapet.

The two figures below were on the far side of the courtyard and half in shadow, yet there was no mistaking the set of broad shoulders under the white tuxedo, the bare arms wound around his neck. If he was struggling to get away he certainly wasn't putting much effort into it. Lauren pushed herself back from the sight with hard and hasty hands. She felt physically sickened. Well, he had warned her, hadn't he? Francesca was not to be resisted.

'It means little, I am sure,' comforted Donata at her side. 'Nicholas is . . .'

'Is like any other man,' Lauren finished for her. 'Do you know who that woman is?'

'I believe she came with Roberto Emanuele, if it is the one I am thinking of.'

'It is.' Lauren added tautly. 'She was Nick's mistress for two years.'

'Ah!' There was sympathy in the exclamation. 'That is another matter.' The dark brows creased suddenly. 'But then how is it that she arrives with the Emanueles?'

That, thought Lauren grimly, was the thousand dollar question, and one to which it was doubtful she would ever have an answer she could believe!

She kept out of Nick's way for the rest of that interminable evening, nursing her hurt. Donata's philosophical acceptance of male infidelity was all very well when there was no depth of emotion involved, but would she have felt the same way had their positions been reversed?

Signor di Severino had disappeared from the gathering some time before. Finding him in the small salon to which she went in the hope of finding a little privacy for a few minutes took Lauren aback.

'I'm sorry,' she said from the doorway. 'I didn't realise anyone was in here.'

'That need not stop you from joining me in retreat,' he responded as she started to close the door again. 'It will be two hours or more before our guests begin to leave.'

It was an invitation not a command, but Lauren didn't have it in her to refuse. There was a window close by, the shutters left open on the night. She went to look out at the lighted windows across the canal, hearing the slap of water against the stone below her feet, the distant sound of a motor. The glass held a faint reflection of the room behind her: of the man seated by the fireplace, book open on knee. He was watching her, face immobile.

'You are not alone in resenting the presence of that woman here,' he said unexpectedly. 'What interests me more is how and where the two of you previously met.'

So he had overheard the exchange, Lauren thought. But then Francesca had fully intended that he should. She took her time in turning, propping both hands behind her against the sill to take her weight.

'It was at a party in Rome,' she said. 'She was there with her husband.'

'Luigi Bardini.' The faintest of smiles crossed his face as her expression altered. 'I have made it my business to know the details of my grandson's affairs—in every sense of the word. There were others before that one out there. Do you think to change a man of his appetites?'

It was a moment before Lauren answered. When she did . speak it was with flat intonation. 'From what Donata tells me I shouldn't even want to change him.'

'But you are not Donata.'

'No.' She lifted her shoulders. 'It's a bridge I'll have to cross if I come to it.'

'You will come to it. There is nothing more certain.' He paused, expression softening a fraction. 'I have no quarrel with his choice of a bride, only with his reasons for marrying at all.'

'Were your reasons for wanting him to marry Fiorella Bianchi really any better?' Lauren responded levelly.

'I believe so. The dilution of the di Severino blood was a bitter pill to swallow, but an Italian bride would at least have balanced the scales a little. In your children Nicholas's Italian blood will be even further diluted.'

'We may not have children.'

His brows lifted. 'You do not wish it?'

Lauren bit her lip. That kind of lie was beyond her. 'Yes,' she admitted. 'So does Nick. But that doesn't mean it has to happen.'

'For two healthy young people—which I am sure you both are—there is little doubt.' He shook his head, mouth wry. 'I must reconcile myself, must I not?'

'I understand how you must feel, *signor*.' The words were torn from her. 'And I sympathise. But what can I do?'

'If you have to ask,' he said sorrowfully, 'then your power is too limited to be of any use to me.' He closed the book on his knee with care, pressing himself slowly to his feet. 'It is time I said goodnight to our guests.'

Lauren remained where she was as he left the room, heart heavy as lead. The assessment had been only too accurate; even Francesca had more power than she did. If loving someone could cause this amount of pain was it worth it anyway?

She had her answer to that question at least when Nick reached for her that night, her planned protests dying in her throat at his first possessive touch. In spite of her jealousy, or perhaps even in some obscure way because of it, her response had never been so swift, so intense, so utterly and totally complete.

'You're two different people,' he murmured huskily

when they lay boneless and exhausted in the aftermath. 'Cool and collected and typically British by day, and a wild woman by night! How could someone with your capacity for enjoying sex wait so long to experience it?'

'Because it took someone like you to show me what I needed,' she said with only a faint edge. 'I suppose I should be grateful for all the practice you had in the past. It's supposed to make for perfection.'

There was a smile in his voice. 'Is that what I provide?'

Her own smile had no humour. 'I'll let you know better when I've a basis for comparison.'

It was difficult to judge his true reaction in the dark. His laugh sounded normal enough. 'That's a dangerous statement to make.'

'You mean no wife of yours had better look at another man?'

'It's one way of putting it.' He kissed her lightly and eased himself away, turning her round to fit her against the hard curve of his body, one arm heavy across her waist. 'Go to sleep, *amante*.'

Lover. He had called her lover. A long way from love, perhaps, but comforting nevertheless. The moment to tax him with that meeting in the courtyard had come and gone. It was too late now. What she had to do was make Francesca a poor second best.

The party was split between three cars for comfort. Nick had refused the services of a chauffeur, preferring to take the wheel himself. Seated in the rear with Donata who had elected to accompany the two of them, Lauren viewed a landscape not unlike the Cotswolds in appearance, with thickly wooded slopes rising gently from the plain. Here and there the tall bell tower of a church signalled the presence of a village, the occasional stately villa providing contrast. A gentle land, already beginning to turn brown beneath the relentless rays of the sun.

'The Berico hills,' said Donata. 'From Valdagno we have only a few kilometres to travel—we shall be at the villa in time for tea.'

And tomorrow the ceremony, thought Lauren, eyes on the back of Nick's head. The crisp line of dark hair made her stomach muscles curl, her fingers itch. She wanted to lean forward and slide her arms about his neck, to put her lips to the smooth cheek. She was his wife now; no additional ceremony could make her feel more so. Yet she was glad it was to take place.

The road was climbing now, the slopes to either side embroidered with woods and vineyards. There were glimpses of distant snow-capped mountains—the Dolomites, Lauren reckoned, dredging up her schoolgirl geography. A small, old-fashioned train followed a track which paralleled the road at several points, its progress punctuated by shrill squeaks on what sounded like a policeman's whistle. Rounding a bend to see the track meandering carelessly between the gardens of a group of dwellings, it was easy to understand the necessity for a noisy approach.

Rivago was more of a small town than a village, its long, straggling main street lined with shops and cafés. They passed the eighteenth-century church on the way out, driving for another kilometre or so before at last turning in between opened iron gates to run through rich vineyards. The first sight of the villa itself left Lauren gasping. It was Palladian in design, its vast and imposing entrance portal supported by four stone pillars rising the full two storeys high. Life-sized figures carved in stone topped the structure, complementing those grouped about the fountain which lay at the centre of the curving cobbled driveway. Fine lawns stretched to either hand, fronted by flower beds vivid with colour.

'Comfortable little place, isn't it?' said Nick satirically, bringing the car to a smooth halt before the wide expanse of steps.

Lauren could only agree with the implied criticism. The villa was an architectural triumph but in no way a home. She went with Donata up the steps, glad that they were well ahead of the rest of the party. She needed time to come to grips with the sheer magnificence of her surroundings.

The huge central hall had wide corridors leading from it to all four quarters of the building. Off these opened the living rooms, each one a designer's set piece. No child had ever been given the run of such a house.

'We had our own quarters,' Donata confirmed when Lauren put the question. 'As children we came downstairs for meals only on special occasions. We did not feel deprived. There is a swimming pool at the rear, and a whole stable of horses. Later, when you return for the summer, you will enjoy both.'

Nick was still back in the hall talking to one of the staff. Lauren said questioningly, 'The summer?'

'The womenfolk always leave the city during the hotter months.'

'But not the men?'

'Only at the weekends,' Donata smiled a little at the expression on Lauren's face. 'It has always been that way.'

'Not any more,' Lauren declared firmly. 'I stay where Nick is!'

'Because you do not trust him to be alone?'

There was that too, it had to be admitted. Especially while Francesca remained in Venice. The very thought was a cloud on the horizon. 'Where will you be?' she asked.

'Perhaps with you here. It will depend on Filippo's whim. He has no property outside of the city himself, so he may well prefer that I continue to come to Rivago where he can join me when he wishes.'

'One of the perks?' Lauren shook her head at the look of inquiry on her companion's face, already regretting the remark. 'Forget I said anything. Like you keep telling me, I just don't understand the system.'

The other cars had arrived. She went to meet her father, smiling at his expression.

'You haven't seen anything yet!'

'I've seen enough to realise it isn't going to be easy to live with,' he said. 'You're not cut out for any of this, Lauren. A cottage in the country, a couple of children and a husband you can rely on, that's your style.'

How well he knew her, she thought. She said softly, 'You're not suggesting I can't rely on Nick?'

'To stay faithful?' Hugh Devlin shrugged. 'Italian men are notoriously hot-blooded.'

'Except that Nick is only half Italian.'

'And too male for that to be much of a safeguard.' The hesitation was brief. 'That woman last night— Francesca something or other—she was no stranger to him.'

'She was no stranger to me,' Lauren replied lightly. 'I'm not afraid of her.'

'Then you should be,' came the response. 'Her kind is recognisable in any language. She won't give up easily.'

Green eyes met his, determination in their depths. 'Neither will I!'

# CHAPTER TEN

COFFEE that evening was taken out beneath the wide, covered terrace at the rear of the villa, the whole group comfortably disposed around the padded cane chairs and sofas. The pool was set into a further sunken terrace, its surface floodlit. Lauren would have loved a dip, but no one else seemed inclined to suggest it and she lacked the nerve to do so herself.

The service next day was to be at eleven in the morning, that much she already knew. The realisation that it was to be held not at the church they had passed in Rivago itself but at the private chapel right here on the Estate had come as a surprise, yet not an unpleasant one. She was wearing cream for the ceremony not white, which fact might have given rise to some certain speculation among the villagers who would no doubt have turned out to see the bridal pair. Cristina had said that only the immediate family and senior members of the house staff would be present. On Sunday they would all of them return to Venice, her father directly to the airport.

His own marriage to Carol was still arranged for the end of the month. Lauren had extracted a promise from Nick that they would both attend.

'He can give you the cheque at the same time,' she had added in the privacy of their bedroom while they were dressing for dinner. 'Unless something drastic happens during the next couple of weeks, those shares are going to be paying huge dividends.' She hesitated, watching Nick's face. 'I'm sure he'd welcome any suggestions as to what he should do with the profits. The whole business has him tied up in knots!'

'It's a decision he has to make himself,' came the level response. 'He could allay some guilt by giving it to a deserving charity.'

'Even though it's tainted money, so to speak?'

Nick's smile was dry. 'They wouldn't know that— probably wouldn't care too much anyway providing there was no chance of a come-back. Personally, I don't care if he decides to keep it himself. He's gone through enough for it.'

'He won't do that!'

'Well then.' He shrugged. 'He's a grown man. Leave him to it. His job is safe whatever he does.'

'Thanks to you,' she said softly. She paused again, thoughts veering off on a different track. 'When do you plan on resigning your place on the Board?'

'I don't,' he said. He was concentrating on the bow tie through the mirror, not looking in her direction at all. 'Not yet, at any rate.'

Lauren stared at him, unable to stay the sudden small leap of hope. 'You're going to find it something of a strain surely?'

'Initially perhaps, until I've caught up with things here. Vincenzo and his father do the actual work, remember. I only have to know what's going on.'

The hope died as swiftly as it had arisen. She said wryly. 'That's the way it's supposed to be. I can't see you as a mere figurehead.'

His smile was faint. 'You may be right at that. Let's wait and see.'

I want to go home! she had a sudden desperate urge to cry, but she bit the words back. Home was supposed to be wherever the heart was, and hers was undeniably here with this man she had married. She had to find consolation in the knowledge that he would be commuting on a reasonably regular basis. Nothing or no one was going to stop her from going with him, she told herself fiercely.

'Do you feel like a walk?' he asked now, bringing her back to the present. He was already on his feet, holding out his hand to her in the rightful assumption that she would not be refusing the offer.

Lauren rose gladly, comfortable in the knowledge that her father was enjoying a conversation with Stefano Laurentiis. The two of them got along very well.

'It's going to seem strange when Dad goes back on Sunday,' she observed lightly when they were out of earshot of those left on the terrace. 'I'll miss him.'

'It's only going to be a couple of weeks before you see him again.'

'I know. All the same. . . .' She left the rest unsaid, sensing a certain lack of sympathy. 'How long do you think we'll be able to stay in London?'

'No longer than necessary.' His tone was short. 'I still have a lot to catch up on here.'

'But you'll need to spend some time on your own affairs.'

'These *are* my own affairs.'

'You know what I mean.'

'Too well.' He was strolling with hands thrust into trouser pockets, the distance between them wider than it had been a moment or two previously. 'Don't run away with the idea that I'm going to find it impossible to leave again once I'm there, because it won't happen. You'll be tied up yourself when we get back, helping with arrangements for Donata's wedding.'

If there had been any camaraderie before there was certainly little left now. 'Considering the way you feel about arranged marriages,' she said on a brittle note, 'I'm surprised you want any involvement at all.'

'I might prefer to do my own choosing,' he said, 'but that doesn't mean I'm against the general idea. Can't you get it through your head that things are different here!'

'You mean most marriages are contracted without love? You don't have to underline that fact for me! We're a perfect case in point, aren't we?'

The answer seemed a long time in coming. When he did speak it was dispassionately. 'You don't appear to miss the emotion so very much.'

Miss it? Her throat hurt. She said huskily, 'I'm not complaining. There are a lot of women would gladly exchange places with me, I'm sure.'

'Just as a lot of men would give their eye-teeth to be in my position,' came the sardonic retort. 'Especially at night!'

'Is that all you can think about!' She had stopped in her tracks, torn by an anger she needed to vent. Her eyes blazed as she looked up at him, so tall and strong and untouchable, her lips forming the words for her. 'You don't imagine your inimitable technique is the only reason I'm staying with you?'

He was very still, expression grimly controlled. 'I can't think of any other. You hate it here.'

And that was as much as it meant to him. Lauren drew a painful breath. 'Not as much as I did. It's a lifestyle one can adjust to without too much effort. Why else do you think I haven't mentioned Francesca again?'

The grey eyes were cold as ice. 'You tell me.'

'Perhaps I decided sharing your favours was a small enough price to pay for what I was gaining on the practical side!'

She had overstepped the limit; she could see that in the way his whole body stiffened, his hands coming slowly out of his pockets with an implied threat that turned her urgently on her heel.

They were in the topiary garden, the dark shapes of bush and tree looming everywhere about them, creating shadows that made it impossible to see where the path went to. The first curve caught her unawares. Only her frantic grab at the nearest bush saved her from measuring her length across the sharp jut of the edging stones.

Nick was on her before she had time to regain her balance, yanking her upright with a hand like iron and dragging her along with him until grass sprang beneath their feet. She went down like a ninepin under his weight, robbed of the breath to make any verbal protest beyond a strangled sob of mingled fury and fear. The dress she was wearing was made of flimsy cotton voile; it ripped like paper under his steely fingers. Lauren caught her lower lip between her teeth, steeling her body for what was surely to come, her eyes wide and dark as she gazed up into the ruthless features. She had asked for retaliation of some kind, but not like this!

The anger drained from him suddenly, his face expressing a wave of self-disgust. He pushed himself roughly away from her, kneeling in the grass with his chin on his chest and his breathing ragged. Lauren rolled on to her side, the knuckles of one hand pressed against her lips as she fought to collect herself. It hadn't happened, that was all that mattered right now. It hadn't happened!

She quivered when he touched her, resisting the longing to turn and throw herself into his arms. Confessing her feelings for him now could only make matters worse.

'I'm sorry,' he said on a low gruff note. 'That wasn't called for.'

Lauren forced herself to look at him, seeing the regret in his eyes with a slight easing of the tension gripping her chest. 'I shouldn't have said what I did,' she murmured. 'That wasn't called for either.'

The smile only touched his lips. 'Perhaps I deserved it. Why shouldn't you weigh things in balance?'

'It wasn't. . . .' Lauren began, her voice petering out as he shook his head.

'Let's just forget about it, shall we? We each know where we stand.' His glance dropped to take in the state of her dress, the wryness increasing. 'We'd better make our way round to the front entrance and hope we're not seen. I'd hate to try and find a plausible excuse for the way you look.'

So, thought Lauren numbly, would she. Nick's refusal to listen to her explanation hurt, but there was little she could do about it, except hope that he wouldn't take the statement itself too much at face value. There was no adequate compensation for Francesca.

They gained the privacy of the bedroom allocated to them without meeting anyone. The elbows of Nick's tuxedo were grass-stained, and he hadn't brought a spare.

'It's all right,' he said without concern. 'They'll clean it for me downstairs.'

'Imagining what?' asked Lauren, drawing on a wrap, and he shrugged.

'It isn't important what they imagine. What are you going to do with the dress?'

'Hide it until I can get rid of it,' she said, and couldn't resist the rider. 'After all, it isn't the first time you've ripped a dress of mine!'

'No,' he agreed. 'It may not be the last either if you keep reminding me of it.' He studied her for a moment, expression austere. 'We both have to learn forbearance, and not just in one sense of the word.' His gaze switched briefly to the twin beds. 'Perhaps we should start tonight.'

Pride swamped any protest on Lauren's part. If he wanted to prove to her that he for one could manage without their lovemaking, then she wasn't going to argue about it. 'Let's,' she said.

They finished preparing for bed in silence, each busy with their own thoughts. Lauren wondered dully if Nick's were centred on Francesca. It was even possible that she was the reason he didn't want to sleep with her tonight. The other woman had held him for two whole years—would perhaps have held him still if she'd been content to accept her position in his life. The fact that it had been, and probably still would be, a purely physical relationship was no comfort at all because their own was little more.

The single bed felt strange, and singularly lonely. Lying there in the darkness listening to Nick's regular breathing, she wished she were only capable of the same degree of detachment. Her body ached to be with him. Yet the frenzy of the past week could scarcely be sustained indefinitely, she told herself in an attempt at comfort. There was just the faint chance that Nick was genuinely tired, especially after that bout of sheer fury outside. Anger itself was a draining emotion.

She had thought him asleep. His sudden jerking back of the covers caused her heart to jerk. The rising beat in her ears almost drowned the sound of his movement. Only when he slid beneath the sheet at her back did she become certain of his intentions.

'My willpower isn't what it should be,' he murmured

gruffly in her ear as his arms came about her. 'Not where you're concerned, at any rate! Turn round, Lauren. Don't make me eat humble pie.'

She turned at once, arms sliding around his neck, lips blindly seeking. 'You couldn't eat humble pie if your life depended on it,' she whispered against his mouth. 'I wouldn't even try to get at you that way.'

'Which makes you a great deal less vindictive than I am.' His tone was rueful. 'I've always been the one in charge of the time and place. It isn't easy to accept any different order.' He put his lips to the vulnerable hollow of her throat. 'Bear with me, will you? One day we'll both feel the same way.'

So he had guessed. Lauren felt few regrets. It would be a relief not to have to hide it any more. All the same, she found it difficult to say the actual words without feeling that she was begging for some like return. When they could both of them say them and mean them, that would be the time.

The little chapel was full of flowers. Standing there at Nick's side listening to the words which needed no translation, Lauren told herself she had never been happier. The night just passed seemed like a dream, except that she knew it had all been real. The image of Francesca had been relegated to a distance. Nick didn't need her. Not any more. She would make sure he never needed anyone else ever again.

Coming out into the bright sunshine, she caught Donata's eye, envying the true serenity she saw there. It must be wonderful to be so certain, so sure of one's way. Not for her the agony of wanting, of needing to hear the spoken words of love. She stood secure in what she had.

The day moved smoothly onward. Signor di Severino

made a visible effort to sound sincere in his congratulations, but the strain was there in his eyes. Lauren knew it was useless asking Nick to reconsider his decision; it was hardly fair to expect that he should be prepared to turn his back on his entitlement. His needs had to be her main concern, not those of others. She loved him and she would stick by him, whatever he chose to do.

'Happy?' asked her father softly when he managed to corner her alone for a moment of two after the superb luncheon.

'Deliriously,' she acknowledged. Her smile backed up the statement. 'The civil ceremony was so impersonal. I didn't realise just how different I was going to feel today.'

He was smiling too. 'I'm relieved. You know, when you first passed the news on I wasn't sure what to think—especially after Carol told me the circumstances. I couldn't believe there wasn't some kind of ulterior motive. Maybe I should apologise to that husband of yours for misjudging him.'

'He'd only shrug it off,' she said, studiously ignoring the pang. 'We're coming over for the wedding, Dad. Are you planning on going anywhere afterwards?'

'We haven't got round to deciding,' he admitted. 'Too many other things to think about. You'll stay at the house anyway, won't you? No point in going to an hotel when there's three bedrooms going begging.' He paused, tone altering a little. 'I'm considering putting the place up for sale after the wedding. It's a bit large for just the two of us.'

It was only because she had grown up in the house that she felt so stricken by the thought, Lauren told herself, and knew that wasn't the whole truth. Her old home would have provided a familiar base to use on their visits to England—an odd kind of security.

'You might not stay two,' she responded lightly. 'Stranger things have happened!'

He laughed. 'I think we're both just a bit past starting a new family. We'll leave that to you and Nick. He wants children, doesn't he?'

'Oh, yes.' Lauren saw no reason to underline the pressing reasons for that desire. 'We both do. Carol will hate being called Grandmother!'

'Nonsense. She'll love it! You won't be able to keep her away—always providing we'll be invited, that is.'

'You'll be invited. Has Carol ever visited Venice?'

'Not that I know of. I think she'd have mentioned it over the last couple of days or so.' There was just a hint of irony in his tone.

'Father and daughter doing well?' asked Nick, joining them. The arm sliding about Lauren's shoulders had a possessive feel, almost as if he wanted to remind her where her loyalties now lay. 'Grandfather asked me to convey his apologies for an early retirement, but he needs his siesta.'

'Is he all right?' Lauren queried swiftly. 'I mean, apart from feeling tired?'

'That's all he'll admit to.' Nick looked back to Hugh Devlin. 'Lauren will have told you my grandfather is a sick man?'

'Yes.' There was a faint constraint still in the older man's manner. (It would, Lauren reflected wryly, probably always be there, considering the circumstances.) 'Apparently there's nothing that can be done.'

Nick said dryly, 'Some things even money can't buy. My aunt would be delighted if you'd ask her to show you the gardens, by the way. She finds you very congenial company for an Englishman.'

'Was that really necessary?' murmured Lauren on a reproachful note as her father went willingly to comply with the request.

Dark brows lifted. 'You think Miss Gordon might object?'

'I didn't mean that.' Green eyes searched grey, looking for signs of mockery. 'What you said about some things money can't buy.'

'Oh, that.' He shrugged, expression unrepentant. 'As a matter of fact it wasn't intended as a jibe in his direction.'

'You didn't make that very clear.'

'I didn't feel the need. One thing I refuse to do is tiptoe round other people's emotions.' He put out a swift hand as she made to reply, one finger tip coming to rest lightly against her lips. 'We're not going to argue today of all days, are we?'

Lauren relaxed, smiling back. 'No, of course not.'

'Good.' The finger tip had moved along the line of her cheek, the caress stirring her senses in the same familiar fashion. He knew it too. It was there in the grey gleam of his eyes as he added softly, 'I'm sure no one is going to complain if we decide to take our siesta early too. Tonight there will be a lot of new people to meet—for both of us. We'll need to be well rested.'

Her laugh came low, the hurt forgotten. 'Is rest what you have in mind?'

'Eventually,' he said.

Afterwards Lauren was to remain ever convinced that their child was conceived that same afternoon. They made love as if for the first time, building slowly from a simple touching of lips to a peak where nothing else existed but the single primitive urge.

Wakening from the deep sleep of utter repletion to the early evening glow, she found it difficult to distinguish dream from reality in her mind. The words 'I love you' still lingered with an almost audible clarity, yet with no indication as to who might have said them, or when. Dream or no, she decided in the end, they were an omen for the future. One day there would be no doubt.

The dress she was to wear that evening was dark blue in colour and designed Grecian style to leave one shoulder and arm completely bare. With her hair swept up into smoothly gleaming coils to one side of her head, she looked, Nick said, like Athena herself!

Signor di Severino presided over the gathering. Watching him during the course of the evening, Lauren could see the deterioration in one short week. She wished she could get a little closer to him, but realised the futility in even trying. To him she symbolised the end of an era. While he may not dislike her on a personal basis, he would never forgive her for ruining his one slender hope.

Although coming along, her Italian was not yet good enough to hold more than the most simple of conversations. Lauren lost count of the number of times she apologised for her failure to comprehend all that was said to her.

'I feel bad asking people to say it again in English,' she confessed ruefully to Nick at one point when they happened to be alone together for a few minutes. 'Especially when they don't all speak the language.'

His laugh made light of the problem. 'You're learning all the time. No one could expect you to be fluent so quickly.' He paused, looking at her with a taunting gleam. 'Do you know what they *are* saying about you?'

She pulled a face, laughing back. 'I only want to know if it's flattering!'

'Oh, it is. They're saying that my taste is impeccable—although my Italian half naturally takes full credit for that.' His tone softened. 'I like being the object of envy when it comes to my fellow men. It's good for my ego.'

'As if,' she came back lightly, 'it needed any boost!'

His lips slanted. 'You take so much at face value, *cara*. Things aren't always as they seem.'

Lauren would have liked to pursue that statement further, but with others descending on them now was not the moment.

It was after two o'clock when the last of the guests departed. Nick was to drive Lauren and her father straight to the airport after breakfast, leaving the rest of the party to return to the Palazzo in their own time.

'We'll leave around ten-thirty,' he said as everyone began to drift away to bed. 'No sense in cutting things too fine.'

'No sense at all,' agreed Hugh. His gaze lingered on his daughter, wry acceptance in his eyes. 'See you both later then.'

Impulsively she leaned forward to kiss him on the cheek. 'Goodnight, darling.'

Nick waited until they were moving away up the staircase before saying softly, 'It never occurred to me that a father might find it so difficult to accept the loss of a daughter. One day I may be called upon to make the same sacrifice.'

There was security in the thought of that distant future. Lauren's heart felt light. 'We'll stick to sons,' she declared, 'and spare you the anguish. I'm sure Dad would agree they're far less trouble!'

The smile touched his eyes as well as his lips. 'I doubt he ever complained.'

He took her in his arms the moment they were inside their own door, kissing her into mindless abandonment. At which point they shed their clothing she was never sure. All she remembered was the warmth and the weight, the scorching flame of his lips, the giving and taking until there was nothing left but that final tumbling drop into oblivion.

They made the airport with an hour to spare. Hugh didn't want them to wait, but Nick insisted.

'We'll be over the day before the wedding,' he said at the gate when the flight was eventually called. A smile crossed his lips. 'Donata will make three in a row. It seems to be catching on.'

Lauren was quiet in the launch Nick had hired to take them across to Venice. Her father would be in the air now, heading back to familiar places. Viewed from this end, the two weeks before they could join him seemed an age. Even then it would not be for long.

'The others won't be home before evening,' remarked Nick casually as they passed under the final bridge of the Rio Dell Arsenale into the Pool of St Mark's. 'Would you like to stop by the Piazza for a drink?'

'I'd love it,' she said, brightening a little. 'But won't it be too crowded at this time of day?'

'It's crowded any time of day right now. You'll need to wait for the winter months to see it free of tourists.' He leaned forward to speak to the helmsman, sitting back again as the latter veered the boat from its present heading towards the long row of gondolas moored along the front of the Doge's Palace and Piazzetta.

Lauren caught a glimpse of the Bridge of Sighs as they passed the end of the Rio di Palazzo. So far there had been little opportunity to plumb the history of the place in any depth, but she would have time and to spare in the coming months. Many would envy her that experience. Why couldn't she accept it as such? Without Nick there was nothing for her back home anyway.

There were representatives of almost every nationality under the sun in Venice that day judging from the many and varied accents overheard in passing. The Japanese seemed to proliferate, clicking away with Canon and Pentax at anything and everything; gathering into inscrutable little groups to have snapshots taken from all angles.

'Dedicated travellers, the Orientals,' observed Nick, steering Lauren around the back of a circle all standing - with heads bent far back as they craned to follow the pointing finger of the guide in their midst. 'I spy a free table across the way!'

They beat another party to it by a short head. Nick summoned a waiter with a flick of a finger, ordering coffee for them both. The sun was hot, the noise overpowering, yet the atmosphere was undeniable. From where she sat, Lauren was looking directly at the Basilica, standing like a huge ornate altar tipped with gold minarets. Pigeons strutted unconcernedly between countless feet.

'Still feeling out of place?' asked Nick softly, watching her face.

She smiled and shrugged. 'Don't you?'

'I spent most of the summer vacations here while I was a boy, plus a spell in the winter. It's as familiar to me as any other place I've lived.'

'And the Palazzo? That feels like home?'

'Not exactly. But it will. Give it time.'

Their coffee arrived. Lauren watched Nick as he paid the waiter, admiring the healthy gleam of thick dark hair, the smooth warm tint of his skin. Here was a man who drew attention the way a magnet drew iron filings, and he was her husband. She wanted to proclaim that fact to every woman whose head turned his way. Her fingers touched the diamond-studded hoop which yesterday had joined the simple gold band already there. Twice married, and still looking for reassurance. What more did she want?

Someone had halted right behind her chair. Lauren saw Nick's expression change even as she caught the first waft of perfume.

'I thought you were back in Rome,' he said.

'I have other thoughts,' came the smooth response. 'I may join you for a moment, yes?'

Laura steeled herself to stay calm as Francesca moved into view. 'I'd rather you didn't,' she said clearly.

Whatever kind of reaction the Italian woman might have been anticipating this was quite obviously not it. She stood with hand already resting on the back of one of the spare chairs, expression nonplussed. She was wearing a knitted cotton suit of utter simplicity and superb fit, her hair caught back from her face by a bandeau of turquoise silk. She had never, Lauren thought numbly, looked lovelier.

Nick looked from one to the other of them, lips faintly twitching. 'I think she means it,' he said. 'Nice seeing you, Francesca.'

The other said something explosive before turning on her heel and stalking away. Lauren could feel the flags of colour in her cheeks, the trembling in her limbs.

'It's said,' Nick remarked at length, almost conversationally, 'that if one sits in St Mark's Square for long enough the whole world will eventually pass by.'

Green eyes met grey, the spark reciprocated. 'You're trying to tell me that was purely coincidental?'

Dark brows lifted. 'You're suggesting it was arranged?'

Common sense refuted the possibility. She sighed and shook her head. 'No, of course not. You couldn't be sure of coming here this afternoon.'

'Where you're concerned. I can't be sure of very much at all.' The pause stretched between them. When he spoke again it was on a cooler note. 'I think we may as well be on our way.'

There was so much she wanted to say, yet the words refused to come. While Francesca was here in Venice she would know no peace of mind.

# CHAPTER ELEVEN

THE following days were too full to allow much time for introspection. Lauren found herself drawn into the bustle of pre-wedding arrangements, accompanying Donata to fittings, copying endless lists, observing the way Cristina Laurentiis handled the thousand and one details entailed with doubt that she herself would ever acquire the same ability to command. The task of running the household would officially be hers once Nick inherited the title. She could only hope that his aunt would be willing to share the burden, at least for a time.

'You've no idea how much goes on behind the scenes,' she told Nick. 'It isn't just a case of keeping the place running smoothly, it's making sure no part of it is allowed to deteriorate any faster than it has to. That means being constantly alert for any sign at all of flaking paint or crumbling masonry—even for changes in shading on the walls that might indicate damp. Were you here the year the canal rose almost to the level of the first-floor window sills?'

'No,' he admitted. 'But I've seen the Piazza flooded more than once. Venice is sinking, very gradually but very surely. One day a solution may be found.' They were in their room preparing for dinner. He studied her through the mirror as he looped his tie. 'Feeling a little more settled?'

'After you just told me that!' Lauren smiled and lifted her shoulders. 'It takes time to adjust. Ask me in a month or two.'

'In a month or two you'll be in a different position,' he said levelly. 'We both shall. You must have seen the deterioration in my grandfather even since we first arrived.'

'Yes, I've seen it.' She sighed. 'I only wish there was some way of prolonging his life.'

'Because you dread the day I become *Il Signor*?'

She stiffened a little. 'Not only that. I'd like the opportunity to get closer to him.'

'It wouldn't work, even if you had it.' His tone was brusque. 'Once set, his mind remains that way. My mother's experience should underline that much for you.'

She said softly, 'Are you sure she would have wanted you to take up cudgels on her behalf?'

'You think that's the only reason I'm here?'

'It has to be a great part of it.'

'Don't tell me my own mind,' he said, ignoring the fact that he had asked the question in the first place.

Lauren smoothed green silk down over her hips before answering. 'I don't know what your father was like, but your grandfather isn't the only one with a narrow outlook!'

There was nothing loverlike in the grey glance. 'Leave it,' he advised.

It would be a waste of time continuing the argument anyway, Lauren acknowledged, wondering why she bothered at all. Nothing she could say was going to change things. She wondered dryly if Francesca had been able to exert any influence during their time together. Certainly she had not been able to persuade him to marry her, but then that had not exactly been her own decision either. Whether the other woman was still here in Venice she had no idea. She wasn't sure she even wanted to know. What the eye didn't see the heart couldn't grieve over.

Signor di Severino was present at dinner that evening, but it was apparent that there would not be so very many more occasions when he would feel strong enough to leave his own rooms. He ate little, and said even less. Lauren caught his eyes on her more than once during the meal, the expression in them impossible to define with any accuracy. He watched Nick, too, as if he were weighing them both in balance. Perhaps at last he was reconciling himself to the inevitable. Lauren hoped so. It would make these last weeks a great deal happier for him.

Somehow it came as no great surprise to receive the summons to his rooms the following afternoon. She found him standing before the window in much the same stance as on the first time she had seen him, only this time there was no enmity in the gaze he turned her way.

'Sit down,' he invited. 'I thought it was time we spoke together again.'

Lauren obeyed, waiting until he himself had taken a seat opposite before venturing to open the conversation. 'If it's my assurance that I'll do nothing to prejudice the name of di Severino you want, then you already have it.'

He acknowledged the statement with an inclination of his head. 'That much I had taken for granted,' he said. 'You are a young woman of strong will and a great deal too much assertion, but your integrity I do not doubt.' He paused, eyes steady on her face, the gauntness of his own features emphasised by the shaft of sunlight edging in through the window on his flank. 'I brought you here to ask you to do something against which your whole being will cry out, yet ask I must.'

Lauren's heart thudded sickeningly against her rib cage as her mind leapt ahead to form an obvious conclusion. She had been totally wrong, she thought dully. Reconciliation was not a part of the di Severino heritage.

'You want me to leave, don't you?' she said on a low, rough note. 'Without me the problem is halved.'

Once again the white head inclined, this time with a certain admiration. 'Exactly so. Nicholas will not like it, but he will be forced to accept it if it is your choice.'

'But it wouldn't be, would it?' Her tone was bitter. 'It would be yours!'

'For the greater good of the line, yes. There is time yet for my grandson to form an alliance with a good Italian family.'

'With a special dispensation, no doubt, to nullify the marriage he already contracted? You were the one, *signor*, who insisted on a second ceremony!'

The drawn features became impassive. 'A mistake, I agree. I gave myself no time to consider the alternatives. It makes the situation more difficult, but not unrectifiable, as you say. These matters can be arranged.'

'Only if I agree,' she pointed out. Her hands were gripping the arms of her chair so that the knuckles showed white. 'What makes you so sure Nick would let me go?'

'He would not have to know until it was too late to stop you. He and Vincenzo will be late returning this evening. There is a flight in two hours from now on which a seat is already reserved should you decide to take it. Guido awaits my word.'

Lauren stared at him, struck dumb for a moment by the sheer calculation. 'You really expect me to just up and leave this afternoon without a word to anyone?' she got out at last. 'I'm sorry, but that's out of the question!'

The old man shrugged, as if that was the reply he had more than half anticipated. 'Would it still be out of the question,' he said with slow deliberation, 'if I told you that Nicholas was with the Bardini woman only yesterday?'

Silence fell heavily into the room, hanging like a pall between them. Lauren's thoughts were turned inwards, remembering Nick's impassioned eyes when he had made love to her last night; the hard demand of his body. She had put his lack of tenderness down to the harsh words they had exchanged earlier, and done what she could to smooth things out. In the light of what she had just heard, the whole memory took on a different concept. He had come to her from Francesca—the one thing she had told him she would never accept. Not only that, but he had used her to allay his desire for the other woman. Some things could be forgiven, but not that. Not ever that!

The eyes she lifted were veiled, the pain driven deep down where it could not be seen. 'You're right,' she said. 'That makes a difference. I shan't have time to pack everything. Perhaps you'll make arrangements to have the rest sent on.'

'Of course.' Just for a moment there was shame in his eyes, swiftly conquered. 'It is a pity that we could not have met in more conducive circumstances, Lauren, but that is the way of life.'

It was the first time he had ever used her name, to her face at least. She turned away hastily before the bitter words spilled from her lips. 'You can tell Guido I'll be down in ten minutes,' she said on her way to the door.

She saw no one on her journey back to the room she had shared with Nick. Numbly she packed the bare essentials into a small bag, leaving with no more than a brief, unseeing glance around. Guido was waiting in the launch. He said nothing as he took the bag from her, handing her down into the boat with his usual expressionless face.

Sunlight warmed her body as they came out into the Grand Canal, but it couldn't warm her heart. She was going home at last, yet that meant nothing right now. It was going to be a long time before feeling of any kind returned.

Hugh Devlin was waiting at the airport. He said nothing when she first came through the gate, just put his arms about her and held her for a moment.

'Your phone call was a shock,' he admitted when they were in the car. 'I'd imagined you and Nick might have problems, but not quite so immediately. Do you want to talk about it?'

'Not yet,' Lauren acknowledged wryly. 'Do you mind?'

'Of course not. The first priority is rest. I left Carol at the house getting a meal ready. She won't expect you to talk either if you don't feel like it.'

'I know.' Tears prickled behind Lauren's eyelids; she blinked them hastily back. 'I'll feel better when I'm home again. It seems years since I left.'

There was little conversation after that. Looking out of the window as dusk gathered over the familiar scenery, Lauren tried to tell herself it was worth any price to be back where she belonged, but there was no conviction. There was an empty space inside her that nothing could fill.

Carol took one look at her future daughter-in-law's white, exhausted face and bit back any questions she might have intended to ask. The hot soup and newly baked bread she produced was welcome, but Lauren had to turn down the following dishes.

'If you don't mind,' she said, 'I think I'll go straight on up to bed.'

'Of course we don't mind,' Carol said warmly. She hesitated only a second before adding, 'You don't have to worry about anything here. I moved in over the weekend while Hugh was away. It seemed ridiculous under the circumstances to keep two places going.'

Lauren smiled at the two of them. 'Don't look so guilty about it. I think you're quite right. All the same, there's no reason why I shouldn't get the evening meal tomorrow considering you'll neither of you be home before six-thirty.' She kept her tone level. 'I'm going to need help to sort things out.'

Her old bedroom was waiting for her, the curtains ready drawn against the darkness outside, the covers turned invitingly back. Lauren switched out the lights and went to open a window before getting into bed, standing there for several moments looking at the gently waving branches of the silver birch down by the gates. In Venice the lapping of small waves against the stonework had been a constant night-time background: here there was only the breeze and the distant sound of traffic.

It was going to take some getting used to again, she realised, yet it was home in a way the other could never have been. She had to put these past weeks behind her, starting right now, this very minute. The rest of her life still lay ahead.

The morning brought little respite. Carol offered to get a temp up from the pool to stand in for her in order to provide some companionship, but Lauren refused. She had to get used to being self-sufficient, she said.

She had told them both the gist of what had happened but she doubted if they really appreciated her reasons for leaving the way she had. Carol had been swift to assure her that her home was right here in the house with them, but Lauren had no intention of taking her up on the offer. Next week she was going to start looking for another job, and then somewhere to live. She knew too many people ever to need to be alone for long, unless she wanted to be. None of them would even know about her marriage. She might decide to keep it that way.

The weather was superb, Lauren spent the morning out in the garden in her briefest bikini, trying to immerse herself in the latest bestseller, though without too much success. Tired from a restless night, she dozed off in the heat, wakening with a smile on her face until memory wiped it away. When Nick moved into her line of vision she could only stare up at him.

'You're starting to burn,' he said. 'Not very sensible falling asleep in the sun, even in England.'

Lauren was motionless, afraid he would suddenly vanish if she stirred a limb even while her every sense told her he was real flesh and blood.

'How did you get here?' she asked ridiculously at last, and saw his faint sardonic smile.

'Like any other angel, I flew. Is that the only welcome I'm going to get?'

It took every ounce of willpower she had to stop herself from responding to the invitation the way he obviously anticipated. She sat up slowly, reaching for the bikini top she had discarded earlier and covering herself from his gaze.

'It's the only welcome I'm willing to provide,' she said. 'Why did you bother to come, Nick? Your grandfather must have told you the reason I left.'

'He told me everything.' The firm lips twisted again. 'Was jealousy sufficient cause to deny me a hearing?'

She was at a disadvantage down here while he

remained standing, yet she doubted if her limbs would be steady enough to hold her just yet. 'Would deny be the operative word?' she asked. 'Or were you planning to preach on the narrowness of a mind that refuses to allow a virile man a mistress in addition to a wife!'

'I deny nothing,' he returned, robbing her of even the faintest hope. The grey eyes didn't flicker. 'It's quite true I was with Francesca a couple of days ago. I'm not asking for forgiveness, simply the opportunity to talk it out.'

'To what purpose?' This time she did make it to her feet, warding off his automatic move to render assistance with a wave of her arm. 'I'd as soon you didn't touch me, thanks!'

'All right, I won't.' From the pitch of his voice he was making every effort to remain calm and reasonable. 'Did it ever occur to you that a man can be with a woman without intimacy taking place?'

'*Some* men and *some* women, yes. Not Francesca, and certainly not *you!*' Her laugh held no element of humour. 'God, I should know!'

'You know nothing, except what you want to believe.'

'I only believe what I've been taught to expect.' She made a small fierce gesture with clenched fist, as if pushing him away. 'Just go back where you came from, Nick. I don't need you!'

'You're my wife, dammit!' He had hold of her even as she started to turn, arm jerking her up hard against him. Face a taut mask, he brought his head down to find her lips, prising them apart with the force of his anger.

Lauren braced herself to stand still in his grasp, refusing to give way even when his fingers tore away the flimsy material covering her breasts. His hands were too supple and experienced not to elicit some reaction from her. She felt the heat, the springing tension; knew the despair of having a body she could not control.

'This is how it all began, isn't it?' she gritted the moment he allowed her to draw breath. 'Except that we're in England now, not Italy. Try raping me here and see what happens!'

He let go of her as if he had been stung, half turning to gaze down the length of the garden at the gently waving tree tops, his breathing ragged. He was wearing a dark silk shirt which clung damply to his back, outlining every ridge of muscle. Irrelevantly, Lauren noted the light jacket slung over the back of the other lounger, the leather carry-all dropped at the corner of the terrace. He had moved on her so quietly, so purposefully, confident of his power to bring her eagerly into his arms. Only it wasn't going to be that way. Not ever again. She had proved that much to him just now.

'I'm going to get dressed,' she said. 'You can please yourself. I wouldn't refuse you a drink before you leave.'

He made no attempt to follow her immediately. Upstairs, she took a quick shower and got into a simple striped cotton dress, thrusting her bare feet into a pair of old sandals. She was making no special effort because Nick was here. Let him see for himself how little she cared.

All was quiet when she eventually went back downstairs. Perhaps he had taken her at her word and left, she thought, standing in the hallway. Well, that was what she had wanted, wasn't it? There was little point in anything else.

Her emotions were torn when he suddenly appeared in the living-room doorway. He was in command of himself again, expression inscrutable.

'You said something about a drink?'

Lauren took a grip on her own mind and body, voice creditably cool and composed. 'What would you like?'

'Make it coffee,' he said.

'All right.' She turned towards the kitchen. 'I'll bring it through.'

She tautened her lips as she heard him moving after her, but made no demur. The large and sunny kitchen was as good a place as any in which to say their final goodbyes. Nick took a seat at the pine table while she busied herself with the percolator. Her fingers felt like thumbs beneath his gaze.

'Instant would do,' he murmured as she sought the lid.

'Not for me.' Her tone was brittle. 'I prefer the genuine article myself!'

'It takes more time,' came the unmoved response. 'I thought you might prefer to save it.'

'It isn't important.' Lauren pressed down the switch and steeled herself to turn towards him. 'Five minutes or fifteen, it will still be the same in the end.'

The smile was narrow. 'That's when you throw me out?'

'That's when I expect you to go,' she corrected. 'There's nothing to stay for.'

'A matter of opinion.'

She gazed at him helplessly, seeing the set of his jaw, the determined glint in his eyes. 'Nick, it won't do any good,' she got out. 'There's too much against us. There always was. Everything else aside. I can't even trust you!'

'You won't allow yourself to trust me.' His shoulders lifted, his expression wry. 'Not wholly without cause, I agree, but . . .'

'With *every* cause!' Lauren shook her head, pressing

her hands over her ears in a gesture she knew was downright childish and not caring a whit. 'I don't want to hear your excuses, Nick! Can't you get that through your head? I'm sick of being used by you—in all senses! Go paddle your canoe somewhere else!'

She had done it again; she could see that in his eyes. She made for the door before he was on his feet, jerking it closed behind her as she ran for the stairs. If he caught her now there would be no drawing back: the anger in him was too intense. Goading him that far had been stupid, and she knew it, yet she had been unable to stop herself from doing it.

There was a key in her bedroom door. She turned it even as he reached the head of the stairs, leaning her back against the solid wood with heaving breath and a heart that threatened to leap from her chest. Without looking, she knew the knob was being turned: pressure was applied, but only briefly and without real intent.

'I'm not breaking down any doors,' came Nick's voice through the wood. He sounded harsh. 'You can't stay in there for ever, and I'll still be here when you do come out. One way or another, you're going to listen to me, Lauren! I'm not leaving until you do.'

She was silent, voice frozen in her throat. After a moment she heard him move away. Only then did her limbs relax their rigidity. It was true she couldn't stay here for ever, but Carol and her father would be home around half-past six. If she had to wait until then she would do it. Anything rather than run the risk of being in Nick's arms again.

The afternoon crept by on leaden wings. There were books to read, but settling down to one was out of the question. Despite the lack of sound from below, she doubted if Nick would have gone. When it came down to strength of will he was on his own. Certainly hers stood little chance against him without help. Her father would supply that. If necessary he would send for the police. There was irony in that thought—the tables turned.

It would be going too far, she was bound to acknowledge. Nick had committed no violence. Not yet, at any rate. Had she any real faith in her ability to keep on repulsing him, she wouldn't be in this position at all. Yet that didn't mean she would consider going back to him either. There was too much against them.

Her window overlooked the rear garden. When the heat grew too much for her, she went to open it, drawing back sharply from the sight of Nick lounging in one of the chairs below. He had stripped off his shirt and lay with arms folded to support his head, his stomach muscles flat and hard beneath the waistband of his slacks. While he lay down there she could escape safely through the front of the house, Lauren realised. Yet where would she go? If it came to that, why should she be driven from her own home anyway?

'You're not doing yourself any good by sticking it out up there,' he observed without opening his eyes. 'Sooner or later you're going to get what's coming to you.'

'What do you plan to do?' she asked. 'Beat me into submission!'

'Nothing so crude.' His eyes were open now and looking directly up at her, although he didn't move. 'Supposing you give yourself a chance to find out?'

'No!' She jerked the casement to with a bang, preferring the heat to the mockery. This was one time he was not going to have things his own way, no matter what it took to convince him.

It was twenty minutes past six when the car turned into the drive. Lauren heard her father and Carol enter the house, the sound of voices from the hallway. The conversation faded after a moment or two, as if the three of them had moved on through to the living room to continue it. She should go down now, Lauren thought, yet she couldn't bring herself to make the effort.

In the end it was her father who came up to her.

'Open the door, Lauren,' he said gently from the other side. 'We have to talk.'

She went to obey, standing back to allow him access without quite meeting his eyes. 'We'll do it right here, if you don't mind. I've no desire to see Nick again—ever!'

'Are you quite sure that's true?' he asked, sounding uncertain himself. 'Shouldn't you at least give him a chance?'

'He's had more than one.' The lump in her throat was threatening to choke her. 'I suppose he's told you it was all a mistake—that he never even touched Francesca!'

'As a matter of fact, he's told me nothing, except that he doesn't intend leaving without you.' Hugh paused, shaking his head. 'Lauren, he must love you a great deal to come after you like this.'

'He doesn't love me,' she responded thickly. 'I'm a weapon to use against his grandfather. Oh, he wants me, I'll grant you that. I stir his Latin blood. So do a lot of other women.'

Her father smiled a little. 'Few men can turn a totally blind eye to an attractive woman, regardless of how deeply they might feel about one particular one. Women, neither, if it comes to that. What counts is what he or she does about it.'

'Exactly.' Lauren made a small hopeless gesture. 'Dad, I made every effort to go along with what he wanted, even though I didn't agree with any of it. I married him for all the wrong reasons in the first place.'

'Possibly. All the same, I can't help remembering the way you looked at Rivago. You knew about this other woman then.'

'I knew she was available again, not that he intended taking up where they left off. She was his mistress for two years.'

'Oh.' His tone had gone flat. 'Yes, I suppose that would make a difference.' He looked at her for a moment, feeling her pain. When he spoke again it was on a hesitant note. 'Lauren, there are times when allowances have to be made—mistakes forgiven. At least talk to him.'

She said gruffly, 'You once said if I had any doubt at all I should come right on home. Are you going back on that?'

'Of course not. It's just that . . .' Hugh paused again, shoulders lifting '. . . just that he seems a different man.'

'He isn't. You can take my word for it.' She attempted a smile. 'I realise it's up to me to get rid of him. All I need is your backing.'

The reply was rueful. 'I've already told him he can stay the night. There's no flight back to Venice before morning anyway. I thought you both needed time to sort yourselves out.'

'It won't do any good, but I understand you can hardly turn round and retract.' Her chest felt tight. 'Sorry about dinner. I was going to have it all ready.'

'Carol's putting something together right now for the four of us.' He waited a moment before adding, 'You will come on down?'

'Yes.' It was going to take every bit of stamina she possessed, but there was no way out. 'Just give me a few minutes.'

It was a far from comfortable evening. Of them all, Nick himself seemed the most at ease. He made no reference whatsoever to private affairs during the meal Carol had prepared so creditably swiftly. Biding his time, Lauren reflected, forcing food down an unwilling throat. Only it wasn't going to make any difference because she was going to make certain he had no opportunity to corner her alone.

To do him credit, he made no special attempt to do so, seemingly content to spend the balance of the evening conversing with her father in desultory fashion. By ten o'clock, she could stand the strain no longer.

'I'm going to bed,' she announced huskily. Green eyes met grey, little wiser for the exercise. 'Goodbye, Nick. I'll expect you to be gone by the time I come down in the morning.'

His shrug seemed to signify acceptance of defeat. 'If that's the way you want it.'

It was, Lauren told herself grimly, *exactly* the way she wanted it!

She clung to that conviction all the way upstairs and into her bedroom. Only when she was alone at last with the door closed behind her did she finally give way to the emotion welling up inside her. She could tell herself she hated the man she had married but it didn't help to fill the void he was leaving in her life. A part of her would always be with him.

The three of them came up together around eleven-thirty. Lauren listened to the muted voices saying goodnight, the quiet closing of doors. Nick was across the landing next to the bathroom: a few yards that may as well have been a thousand miles. They had never been together in spirit; they never would have been. Better to suffer what she was going through now than to lay herself open to further hurt.

Time ticked by relentlessly, monitored by the chiming of the grandfather clock in the hall. Midnight came and went, then, each an aeon later, the quarter hours. Lying there curled into a tight little ball in the lonely bed, she knew that sleep had never been further away.

The hour had almost finished striking when Nick slid in behind her, his hands seizing her wrists as she rolled swiftly on to her back, his weight coming over her to pin her helplessly beneath him.

'You're going to listen to me,' he said in low determined tones. 'I don't care whether you want to or not, you're going to *listen*!'

He was naked; she needed no second sight to tell her that. Her nightdress was too short and flimsy to offer protection from the heat and hardness of him. In spite of everything she could feel her body responding.

'Get away from me!' she hissed on a note of desperation. 'It's over, Nick. I won't let you use me that way any more!'

His mouth shut off the words, fierce though not savage as he kissed her into quivering subjection. 'I said you were going to listen,' he gritted when she finally stopped struggling. 'And by God, you will!' The hands hoding her wrists were relentless, hurting her as he forced them back against the pillows. 'Do you think Francesca can hold a candle to you, you little fool? She's a woman any man could have, providing they offered the right price!'

'So it was purely physical,' Lauren retaliated scathingly. 'Is that supposed to make it all hunky dory again? I don't care why you were with her, it's enough to know you were!'

'I was with her just long enough to tell her she was wasting her time in staying around,' came the ragged response. 'She got the point. I made sure of it.'

Lauren was still, gazing up at him searchingly, trying to believe. 'How?' she demanded.

The smile was fleeting. 'I told her I was in love with my wife.'

'Very convincing.' The hurt was everywhere. 'I'm sure that made all the difference!' She turned her head to one side, afraid he would see the tears that prickled her eyelids. 'Even if it were true it would hardly constitute a reason for depriving yourself of other women.'

'It is true.' The tone was wry. 'Lauren, I realise you don't feel as deeply for me—heaven knows, I've given you little enough incentive—but if we started afresh I could change all that. I need you, *cara*.'

It was the last that got to her. Tremblingly—even now not wholly sure—she freed one hand from his slackened grip and lifted it to his face, tracing the firm line of his mouth with her finger tip. 'Nick, don't pretend with me over this,' she begged. 'I don't think I could take it. I wanted to die when your grandfather told me about Francesca.'

His breath came out in a sigh, as if he had been holding it for a moment or two. 'So he was right after all. You do feel the same way!' The tenderness was there in his voice along with the relief. 'The old devil had us both taped!'

There was more admiration than disrespect in the comment. Lauren said slowly. 'I don't understand. What. . . .?'

'He set us up. He knew if you left I'd be forced into making my choice—and he gambled on what that choice would be.' He rolled to take his weight from her, drawing her with him into the curve of his arms. 'I didn't believe him when he told me you loved me. You're going to have to do some convincing even now. How can you love a man who'd do what I did to you?'

'I don't know,' she said. 'I only know I do.' She put

her cheek down to his chest, feeling the strong beat of his heart. 'Tell me I'm not dreaming this!'

'It's no dream.' He took her hand, guiding it the length of his body. 'Do I feel unreal?'

'No.' She lifted her head again to look at him, the smile still a little uncertain. 'What you said just now about a choice. . . .'

'There wasn't one in the end. You were all that mattered.' His hand smoothed her hair, his touch so gentle she wanted to weep. 'For most of my life I've accepted that I owed it to my mother to step into Grandfather's shoes, but I was wrong. He blighted both their lives by refusing to break an oath, and he's aware of it. Making him pay the way I intended isn't going to alter what's past and gone. I'd have only succeeded in ruining my own life into the bargain.'

'Did you tell him?'

'Of course I told him. I told them all.' He was smiling himself at the memory. 'They send their regard—especially Donata. We're expected back for the wedding, if not before. Vincenzo said to tell you the changes will not be swift but they will be sure. Lucky Grandfather wasn't there when he said it or he might have started to think he'd simply exchanged one bad influence for another.'

The happiness was growing in her like a spring about to burst from a hillside. She put her lips to his, feeling his immediate and devastating response. 'I love you, I want you and I need you,' she whispered. 'Let me show you, Nick.'

They showed each other: lovingly, vibrantly, the passion more potent than it had ever been. Lying there after the storm had passed, Lauren said dreamily, 'I'm due to wake up now. I always do. Tell me what's going to happen next so I'll know where to start next time.'

Nick laughed, dropping a kiss on the end of her nose. 'What's going to happen next is that we start looking for a place to live.'

She snuggled closer contentedly. 'We could always live here.'

'With your father? I hardly think. . . .'

'I meant just the two of us. He's thinking of selling the house.'

There was a pause before Nick said slowly, 'Does it mean a lot to you?'

Something in his voice drew her head up. She looked at him for a long moment before answering. 'No, it doesn't. It was just a passing thought. Where would you like to live?'

He smiled, hand curving her neck. 'I always fancied a place in the country. Somewhere I could keep a couple of dogs. Maybe. . . .' He paused, eyeing her quizzically. 'Why so surprised?'

'Bemused would be closer,' she said. 'Do you remember the afternoon my father arrived when your aunt had to ask me twice if I wanted more tea?'

'Yes, I remember.' His tone had softened. 'You were sitting there with such a far-away expression on your face. I felt shut out, and I didn't like it.'

'You had no cause. It was you I was thinking about. You, and a house in the country with a couple of dogs and . . .' it was Lauren's turn to pause, her muscles turning to jelly at the look in his eyes '. . . Nick, you still want children, don't you?'

'I want everything,' he said. 'All you can give me.'

'And you'll be . . . satisfied?'

The smile came again. 'You're asking me if I'm going to need other women?'

Her gaze didn't flinch. 'You don't find it all that easy to turn away.'

'Some women don't make it all that easy.' He studied her with wry expression. 'You saw me with Francesca the night of the ball, didn't you? I guessed as much from the way you reacted later at the Villa. It was guilt as much as anything that made me lose control.' His lips slanted. 'I don't have any excuses. She was there and the moon was out—and she looked very inviting.'

'And you're a man, and you have Latin blood in your veins, and what else could you do?' Her tone was light but there was no disguising the tremor. 'I'm going to have to watch myself or I'm likely to turn into a jealous shrew!'

The grey eyes were steady. 'You'll have no cause. I may look at other women—I may even feel tempted on occasion—but that's as far as it will go. I love you, Lauren. Only you. That's all you have to remember.'

There were going to be times when it would hardly be enough, she knew that already. Trust had to be learned. Yet if he had been a different kind of man she wouldn't be here in his arms right now, and that was something she wouldn't want to have missed.

'I'll remember,' she said.

# Harlequin reaches into the hearts and minds of women across America to bring you

# *Harlequin American Romance* ™.

# YOURS FREE!

# Enter a uniquely exciting new world with

# *Harlequin American Romance* ™·

**Harlequin American Romances** are the first romances to explore today's love relationships. These compelling novels reach into the hearts and minds of women across America... probing the most intimate moments of romance, love and desire.

You'll follow romantic heroines and irresistible men as they boldly face confusing choices. Career first, love later? Love without marriage? Long-distance relationships? All the experiences that make love real are captured in the tender, loving pages of **Harlequin American Romances.**

What makes American women so different when it comes to love? Find out with **Harlequin American Romance!**

Send for your introductory FREE book now!

# Get this book FREE!